Kheira
& Khogee
The Legend Begins

AMANDA EVANS

SUNGATE PUBLISHING

KHEIRA & KHOGEE: The Legend Begins, Book One

Copyright © 2024 Amanda Evans

Published by SunGate Publishing, LLC.
For information, visit: www.sungatepublishing.com

Disclaimer

The universe of *Kheira & Khogee: The Legend Begins* is a purely fictional creation. While it draws on the rich tapestry of science fiction and fantasy genres, the names, characters, places, people, technologies, and cosmic phenomena described within these pages do not reflect current scientific understanding or the realities of our universe. The views and opinions expressed in this book are solely those of the author and are not meant to represent any real individuals, entities, or events. Any similarity to actual events, or locales or persons, living or dead, is purely coincidental and not intended by the author.

Library of Congress Control Number: 2024913258
Hardback ISBN: 978-1-962245-09-8
Paperback ISBN: 978-1-962245-08-1
Ebook ISBN: 978-1-962245-10-4

Printed in the United States of America

Table of Contents

About the Book

Kheira & Khogee: The Legend Begins is a tale of Twin Flames who have been sent on a secret mission to assist in saving the galaxy. Along their journey Kheira loses her memory, and Khogee must assist her with reconnecting to the part of herself she has lost. Together they must work to accomplish their mission, and defeat the agents their parents have sent after them to end their existence.

Author's Note

As you go along with Kheira & Khogee on their journey you will find that their story reads like a play, versus the way a traditional novel is written. The play format of this book was not intentional but instead is how my creativity unfolded into this work of art.

With this novel being written in the style of a play, the below measures have been taken to provide a smoother reading experience:

- A dash (—) is placed at the beginning of a sentence/paragraph to denote a different character speaking.

- Angle brackets (<>) encapsulate all telepathic conversations.

- A pronunciation guide is located after the last chapter.

Thank you for taking the time to read *Kheira & Khogee: The Legend Begins.*

Dedication

To the light that makes my light shine brighter.

Wherever you may be in the galaxies,

thank you for loving me the way you do.

Chapter 1:

Feel Me

—So, tell me, My Light, what was the experience like?

—I'm still processing, Khogee. I'm… Well, I'm not really sure.

—My Light, speak clearly and honestly with me. There is nothing to fear. I know you feel me completely the same way I feel you. Allow yourself to accept the trust that is ours, here waiting and ready for you to lean into.

—Well, Khogee. At first, I felt a surge of energy hit me. I felt your energy in my entire being. Khogee, it's something you have to feel, words don't quite do it justice.

—Do your best to describe what you felt to me, My Light.

—Well, I felt you in and in between every cell of my body. There was a massive amount of energy that surged through my heart chakra pulsating upward, downward, and outward into every one of my energy centers. I could also hear your soul speaking to me. It was unlike anything I'd ever experienced. The experience was completely euphoric!

—My Light, that is an excellent verbal expression of exactly what I feel when your energy vibrates into my heart chakra. Tell me more about what you heard me say!

—I need a minute.

—Don't be afraid of our connection. Don't run from me, My Light. Feel me completely, feel our bond in the depths of your soul —allow it to guide you. To guide you to the truth. You can trust me completely with every single facet of who you are. Now tell me, My Light, what exactly did you hear me say?

—Trust me, I feel you and the trust we share completely, to the depths of who I am. It's just that I'm still nervous about expressing myself fully to you!

—You never have to hide the essence of your soul from me! I will never judge you or turn away from you. Speak your truth to me genuinely, and I will receive you!

—I… I… I didn't hear you say anything, but I could hear you! I could hear and feel your lungs as they inhaled and exhaled. I could hear the silence in your mind. I could hear and feel pain from memories you hide in the corners of your heart. I felt you deep in my soul. I looked into your heart, and within the depths of your waters, I saw my reflection!

Khogee, why are you so quiet?

—I'm sorry, My Light. It's not my intention to make you feel unsure of yourself at this moment. I was simply pondering and receiving your words, taking a moment to feel their meaning. I see in my first eye and feel in my soul that our connection is growing stronger. Our gifts are opening up even more! The more we continue to practice strengthening our soul link, the more our connection will deepen and soon we will be strong enough to go HOME!

Don't you miss home, Kheira?

I can see and feel its essence all around me and I never want to forget its memory! My Light, we will make our way back there; I promise this to you, Kheira. Your current awakening proves to me we are on the right path! As I walk with you more, helping you to remember. As we slowly allow our link to deepen, we will be unstoppable, and home will be but a thought away.

—Kheira, come now, you must be strong! Do. Not. Give. Up.

—Lovely, I can't continue to do this. He doesn't feel me anymore, and doesn't even know I am here with him.

—How do you know this, Kheira? My dear, have patience. You have moved in and out of so many lifetimes, I believe it is you who has forgotten how he feels, forgotten his light. You've associated love with what your eyes take in, just like the others on this planet. You have forgotten the true power birthed within the soul of love's essence. How love restores, how love heals, how unconditional love truly is. If you truly understood this, then you would know that Khogee can never escape the eternal bond forged between the two of you that forever links your souls together. The love he has for you is eternal! Your connection is still there. His love for you has not left him, Kheira, and never will! It is only that his true self has been buried deep within him. Once you find him and the connection is remembered, allow your light, your energy to call forth within him that which has been buried. Your light and your light alone hold the keys he needs! Kheira, you must help him to Awaken! The same way he has done for you in times past.

Remember, how the two of you landed on Planet Kaytoin and you were separated. He searched Planet Kaytoin to no end until he found you. As he felt through the soul link you two share, somehow you had become disconnected from who you are. Disconnected from any remembrance of even knowing you needed to be looking for him. When he found you, he started the process to help you unlock the memories buried deep within and helped you reestablish the connection to who you truly are. All in an effort to bring you home with him.

—Wait! Khogee said the link, our connection, was needed for us to go home together. You say it as if he could have gone without me and…

—Yes, my dear! That is exactly what I am saying! There is no sacrifice Khogee wouldn't make for the one true lover of his soul. You see he could have gone home at any time, but he knew you couldn't make the trip just yet. Not until you remembered who you were and gained enough light to make the journey! His love for you is so vast, so divinely profound, he couldn't fathom leaving you behind, completely lost and disconnected! Remember what he always says to you! We stand as light all on our own with the ability to illuminate darkness in any space, but together our light can facilitate peace in chaos, and bring forth truth to any lost and dying planet! Have faith, Kheira! Stand firm in knowing that no matter how hard this journey may seem, you will succeed. KNOW you will succeed with every fiber of your being.

Now it is time. It is time to go back into yourself and remember, Kheira. Close your eyes, take three deep breaths, be still and allow the memories to live. Now tell me what you see.

—I see us on Kaytoin, sitting on the beach hand in hand. Khogee is asking me about home.

—Kheira, what do you remember about home?

—Just what you've told me. However, I did have the most vibrant and vivid memory last night, while I was taking rest.

—I'm not sure if it was a memory from home or not.

—Tell me what you saw.

—Well, Khogee, I remember walking on the ocean by a lush grove of trees that bore all kinds of fruit: from green peaches to purple pears, to blue-pink watermelon. As I continued walking on the clear purple and green water, I noticed I could see straight to the bottom! But I was unable to enjoy the beauty around me as my mind was full of all kinds of rambling thoughts. Then out of nowhere, a path made of rectangular shapes appeared in front of me, directly on top of the water. Each rectangular shape along this path was actually made of water, but the rectangular shapes felt and looked just like glass. I placed my bare foot on the first rectangle, and as soon as my foot hit the glass the rectangle turned red. As I journeyed further on this path the colors continued to change, not with each step though. I had to walk a certain distance to see the change, and each color required a different distance before I was able to see the next color.

I was most intrigued as to where this path was leading me, I continued and observed the colors as they changed from red, yellow, orange, green, purple, and then to a purplish white-gold color. Once the path under my feet changed to that purplish white-gold color the most magnificent chair I have ever seen appeared! It looked like it was created for royalty, and made of the purest precious metals and gemstones. The colors mimicked those I saw on the path and seemed to follow the same pattern. The legs of the chair were made of pure rubies. As my eyes traveled up the expanse of the chair, I noticed the red rubies continued up to the bottom section of the seat and then faded into yellow sapphires. The back of the chair was made of a combination of precious gemstones, layered on top of one another, blending so elegantly. The first layer started with orange citrines, followed by dazzling emeralds. As my eyes continued to move up, I saw gorgeous sapphires, and the top of the back of the chair was pure amethyst. The headrest of the chair was most elegant, made of pure amethyst, diamonds, and gold. Did I mention the chair was massive? I started to ponder how comfortable it must be, being that the chair is made out of precious metals and gemstones. It was at that exact moment of pondering I heard a very deep audible voice tell me to sit down. I saw no one but heard the voice clear as day. I felt nothing but calmness, light, and love in that moment, no fear or darkness. So, I tried to climb and sit in the chair but I slipped down every time. I heard giggles in the distance, but again saw no one. I heard the voice again, saying 'Why are you climbing when you can fly!'

'Fly?' I said to myself. 'Sure, why not,' I thought. So, I stood in front of the chair, closed my eyes, and visualized myself flying up to the chair, turning around, and sitting down. When I opened my eyes, to my utter amazement, I was sitting in the chair, and oh how comfortable it felt.

Once I was seated, all my thoughts started to clear one by one. I was in a place of complete stillness, present in every way. A true moment of profound internal peace. Once I had reached a state of acceptance and joy the chair started to move. As the chair moved along the glass path made of water, the same exact colors on the path I described to you earlier appeared. Again, the chair had to travel certain distances for the colors to change. Once the path turned a purplish/white/gold color, the chair stopped. It felt like I'd only been traveling for a few seconds. However, when I looked around me to see where I was, the fruit grove was no longer in sight. In front of me was a cottage made of the same water that looked just like the colorful rectangular-shaped water path.

However, there was one difference, I did not have to touch the cottage for the colors to appear. They were all there, like a rainbow flowing in and out of itself. I was completely mesmerized. I heard the same voice I'd heard earlier, the voice that instructed me to sit in the chair. This time the voice told me to come forth, that only the pure of heart may enter. As I walked to the door, I noticed the path was still there and the colors changed with each step, seven steps to be exact. And did not require me to walk a specific distance for each to change. I placed my hand on the doorknob, and in that precise moment, I felt an energy surge through my body shifting my consciousness completely. It is difficult to put into words, but the closest I can describe is that I felt like I was in the stars looking down on a living planet, able to comprehend and understand everything about its past, future, and present simultaneously. As I turned the doorknob and opened the glass door made of water, I gasped! I was again mesmerized by what I saw.

The inside of this cottage was breathtaking and very exquisite! And not to mention extremely large compared to the smaller size I perceived when I was outside. I saw everything on the inside was made of precious metals, gemstones, and the most expensive silks! I then noticed several beings in the room; some green, purple, yellow, and even ombre-colored. My eyes rested upon a being sitting at a table who was pure melanin, darker than your darkest night. His eyes were pure light and twinkled like the stars in the midnight sky. He stood and told me to step forward, my heart is pure and I may enter. I took particular notice of the fact that his lips never moved. Then it dawned on me, this was the exact same voice guiding me on my journey here.

As soon as I stepped my left foot in the door, I noticed I immediately changed! My skin tone matched that of my guide. As I looked down at my attire, I noticed I was adorned in the most elegant lace green dress I have ever seen, with a slit up the left side all the way to my hip! After I finished admiring my dress, along with my beautiful opulent skin, I lifted my head and noticed a different being in front of me whose skin tone matched my guide's. Then he spoke and said, My Light I have been waiting for you to awaken to the fullness of who you are!

Khogee, you will never believe me, but it was you! I immediately felt our souls link, even before we started to deeply gaze into each other's light-filled eyes. Somehow you immediately knew it was my consciousness from another moment in space staring back at you. Then our guide, who I knew in that moment was our master teacher, advised that we must quickly prepare for the next phase of our journey. He began to speak to all of us in the room telepathically. Advising us to take our seats, and close our eyes. He then proceeded to send us all a massive download of information, directly into our consciousness.

As soon as I received the information my body started to involuntarily sway back and forth. The power of the download was so strong it knocked me out of that moment in space, and I awoke back in this reality. Remembering only one word from the download he sent, WAR!

The entire experience was so strange, Khogee. Yet the experience was so real! It felt as if my consciousness was actually there partaking in, and experiencing every part of each moment. Do you know what this place is? Every moment was so familiar to me as if I'd experienced it before. Khogee, why are you laughing? Wait, what are you doing? Why are you standing up now, is it time for us to retreat for the evening? And, why do you keep laughing and not answering my questions?

—My Light, I know exactly where you were and what was going on.

—Okay, so can you sit back down and tell me?

—Well, I would but I need to get a head start.

—Huh, a head-start? What are you talking about?

—Well, you were remembering a secret location where we can meet with our master teacher no matter where we are in the galaxy. The water path you spoke of that resembled glass, the beautiful gemstone-adorned chair made for royalty, and the cottage made of water. This is a very sacred place only those pure of heart can come within. I can't tell you what it signifies, you have to remember on your own. However, if you can catch me, I just might tell you.

—I can't believe you are trying to run from me, I can barely hear you.

—Can you hear me now, here inside your sacred heart space?

—Yes, I can hear you.

—My Light, I will remind you until you never forget, you will always be able to hear me internally. You just have to stop listening with your mind and start listening with your heart. Now come catch me.

—Wipe that smile off your face. You know I'm faster than you, I will catch you.

—Ha! You think you are faster, but can you jump higher and remember how to breathe underwater? I thought you could run faster than me. Why are you so far back there! Remember in the dream you had last night how you were walking on water? Follow me to the ocean. Let's see if you still remember how.

—Wait I don't know…

—Don't think, just allow your soul to fly free. Allow your body to feel all of nature around you, feel the wind on your face, and the water beneath your feet. Be present only in this moment and allow your soul to connect with the soul of the elements. There you go Kheira! I know you can do anything you put your mind to if only you will allow yourself to trust, accept, and believe. Okay, let's see what you will do now that there is a line of water trees in our path. Will you jump over them or run through them and disturb all the fish?

—You sure are talking a lot of trash for a man running away. You just watch me, I'll jump higher than you.

—Okay, I am stopping; this I can't miss.

—Just watch me, I got this.

—Well, we will see now, won't we, Kheira? Make sure you focus, breathe, and just allow your legs to do the rest. Yes, My Light, you are going to clear the water trees keep going! Don't look at me! Focus on what you are doing before you run into the tree.

—OHHH, I told you I could jump higher than you, I am clearing the trees with no problem. I am going up and up and…

KHOGEE, I am not coming back down. What is going on?

—Ha, you are flying, My Light! I have been waiting for you to remember this ability, I so miss our late-night flights and talks.

—Wait! What! Why didn't you tell me we could fly?

—And, ruin this moment? Seeing the joy on your face and feeling the pure elation you feel right now in your heart while rediscovering another gift. Kheira, calm down, I feel you allowing doubt to creep in. Don't allow fear to consume you, and do not forget to breathe deeply, I'll come right up and join you, My Light. I told you this journey is one of infinity. Now take my hand. Let's see how high we can fly.

Chapter 2:

Oneness

— <Kheira, wake up! Kheira, are you there, wake up and talk to me! My Light, do you hear me?>

— <Yes, I can hear you disturbing me out of my rest. It is the middle of the night, why are you not taking rest!>

— <I'm enjoying the beauty of nature. Can't you hear the waves crashing into one another, while the wind is in the background playing a symphony amongst the trees? My Light, look. Can you see the way the stars are putting on a dance, ushering in the full grand beauty of the moon?>

— <Wow, Yes! Actually, I can see and hear everything you are seeing and hearing right now. Khogee, why can I see and hear what you are seeing and hearing?>

— <You are seeing through my eyes, and hearing through my ears! The link to our soul's blueprint is getting stronger, and soon we will be able to move in and out of oneness with only a thought.>

— <What do you mean by us moving in and out of oneness?>

— <It is one of the beautiful gifts we share as a result of our connection. My Light, individually we stand as one, and over time have learned how to merge. This is the reason why you are able to be here in this moment with me, seeing and hearing all that I do. Even though we are currently in two different locations.>

— <How do we accomplish merging?>

— <When you are ready, My Light, you will remember on your own. Until then we will focus on strengthening our connection.>

— <Where are you? I'll come to you.>

— <You tell me where I am, My Light. You are seeing through my eyes at this current moment.>

— <Everything looks so familiar, but I am not quite sure.>

— <Stay present and concentrate. See my surroundings, listen to my thoughts, and come find me.>

— <Ugh, why must everything be a test or a lesson with you! I'm tired and about to continue taking my rest!>

— <Kheira, you make me laugh. You can lie down and close your eyes all you want. I'm just going to keep bothering you until you get back up!>

— <I see you have it in your heart's desire for me to thrash you tonight.>

— <In your dreams My Light, only in your dreams. How about this? I'll send you some energy to ensure you get a deep peaceful night's rest.>

— <It depends on what kind of energy you are sending me.>

— <Trust me and find out for yourself, My Light! Just like we have practiced before, close your eyes, take three deep breaths, and focus solely on me. Once you receive my energy, describe to me how it feels. Let's start on three. One… two… three!>

<Do you feel me?>

— <Yes!>

— <Wonderful, My Light! Now, I want you to describe to me exactly what you feel, and don't hold back a single detail.>

— <I feel warmth at the center of my heart chakra, slowly pulsating orgasmic energy throughout all of my energy centers. I feel such sensual energy moving into my first eye, steadily pushing upward attempting to erupt out through my crown chakra. At the same time, I feel euphoric

energy pulsating in my heart chakra, making its way down into my solar plexus sending euphoric energy into all of my other chakras. Feeling your energy exploding through the energy centers of my body feels like a million lights being born into existence. Bursting into new colors with each intensifying pulse. Each color is unique and different from the next. My entire body feels warm and is being fueled by your energy in a way that feels like eating sweet ripe cherries on a warm day while you slowly lick and suck the cherry juices off my lips.>

— <My Light, you are doing an excellent job describing to me the reaction your physical body and energy centers are having to my energy. Now I need you to tell me how your soul feels.>

— <My soul feels something so deep; I am not sure I can do this feeling justice with mere words. Feeling you in my heart chakra is so intense, so explosive, so pure, every center in my being is stimulated, which has catapulted me into a state of pure orgasmic bliss. I feel you inside and outside of this reality, inside and outside of the illusion of time. This is so amazing! I feel you in every inch of my being. I feel completely raptured inside of you, like my entire being could explode in the greatest pleasure it's ever known. Khogee, My Light, I need you! Come to me! My Light, why must you tease me, are you there still?>

— <Always, My Light! I'm just breathing in every ounce of your essence. I'm going to keep sending you energy until you stop holding back, allow your body, your being to express the depths of the pleasure you feel in your soul! Then, My Light, and only then will I come to you. I want to feel you explode in pure ecstasy through every energy center in your body. From your root chakra to your crown chakra without me physically touching you, I need you to feel what I feel for you so deeply that the energy explodes out of your heart chakra and makes you scream in pleasure!>

— <Khogee, My Light, I…>

— <Kheira, wait! Be silent, don't say another word, and don't move, I'm tuning into the energy around you right now!>

— <Why are you teasing me such, come…>

— <Silence, Kheira! Something is terribly wrong! I feel an energy source in our dwelling that is ancient and very deadly. I don't quite understand, how did they find us?>

—<Who, Khogee?>

— <My Light, I need you to be very quiet and stealthy. Grab your emergency pack, and come to me now. You must get out immediately!>

— <What is going on?>

— <I will fill you in more once we are safe. Just know they are here to end our existence! NOW MOVE!>

—Khogee, wait! Did you just materialize out of nowhere? How?

—No time now. You were moving too slow and I could feel your fear. I knew I had to come get you. Shhh… listen. They are moving, gaining ground quickly and will be in your room soon. We must move now! Come. Embrace me, place your arms around my waist. And no matter what you see, hear, or feel, do not let go.

—I'm scared, I can feel their evil energy now. I can tell they have one solitary objective which they intend to carry out at all costs. Why do they have so much hate toward us?

—Delusion fueled by the right lies breeds fear, which is a breeding ground for hate! Now relax your mind and silence your thoughts. Focus on my heart chakra and I'll focus on yours. I know we haven't practiced this before but I need you to trust me completely. We must get off this planet.

—How?

—Silence, My Light, breathe. Quiet your mind and focus on my heart chakra. I feel your fear, I need you to let that energy go. Feel my love and allow it to help you overcome your fear. Trust me!

—I do. Completely.

—Keep your arms wrapped around my waist and place your first eye on mine. Feel my love encircling you, see the pure light of love coming from my heart chakra and surrounding you! Protecting you where nothing can penetrate. Do you feel me? Yes?

—I'm not sure.

—No words, just action. You must believe, know all is possible and hold onto that knowing. We must place a protection field of light around us to ensure we escape safely. I need you to focus, feel me, feel my love. Now, give me your love in the form of light, the same way I just gave it to you. Do you see the light coming from your heart chakra, engulfing the both of us?

—Yes, I do!

—Wonderful, My Light, you are doing excellent! Now tell me, what do you feel?

—I feel safe, like we floated above all our troubles. I can see the most beautiful pure white light all around us with another layer of light underneath shining so bright! Beautiful colors of blue, yellow, orange, green, red, and indigo. The colors are flowing in and out of one another, absorbing each other and flowing back to shine even brighter in their own space. Wait!

—Breathe. Calm down, I am here with you, I have not left your side.

—I don't understand, I see and feel you here, but as I open my eyes, I see you… We are flying again, look at the beauty of the sky, simply breathtaking. Wow! So, when I was feeling like we were floating above all our troubles, we literally were!

—Kheira, focus! What were you about to say before?

—Sorry, My Light. I am confused, how are you in two places at once? I see you here with me, but I also see you in my first eye, back in my room fighting the most grotesque-looking creatures.

—Describe them to me.

—They are tall, at least seven or eight feet, red from the top of their heads to their ankles with grayish/black feet. They have two rows of fang-like teeth, five eyes, and no ears! Now can you please explain how you are in two places at once.

—While I had you focusing on creating a protection light around us, I created a doppelganger to stay and fight, so we could get away safely. Now enjoy the view until we get to our extraction point.

—We've never been this high before. I'm seeing the beauty of this planet from an entirely different perspective. To see the glowing green, purple, orange, and yellow fish swimming through the ten-foot-tall water trees busting out the top, soaring like a bird into a perfect summersault, and diving back into the translucent ocean floor. It is truly a sight to behold. I hear the symphony being played by nature, the swish of the water against the backdrop of the wind blowing through the trees. It is so peaceful and soothing to the soul. Where will we go?

—Just hold on tight to me, My Light, and do not worry about the next phase of our journey. We will always take care of each other, and we will always be fine! I know you don't remember things in their entirety, but you will. Until you do, My Light, I will be here right by your side to cover you!

—I'm not sure how, but they have tracked us! Look at me, feel my heart space and find peace! Trust me with every fiber of your being. Please, keep your thoughts positive, and whatever you do don't leave this sphere of protection.

—Wait! What are you doing? Don't leave me!

—Kheira! Kheira! Hear me in your heart, feel me in your soul! I am always with you and I'll never leave or give up on you! You are my light and I will defend you at all costs. Kheira! Please, do not deify my request, please get back! You are not ready for this fight.

—You told me I'm ready when I believe. I may not have all of my memories back just yet, but I don't just believe, I know! I trust in you, My Light. I believe in us! And, I know with every piece of me that I am ready to defend us at all costs! I'll fight by your side till the end! As I feel through my entire being without a shadow of a doubt, for us, the end does not exist.

—My Light, you are ready. Get your sphere prepared. You will defend the right. I'll defend the left. They are full of darkness driven by hate. Their energy is strong. Don't underestimate their power or their thirst for blood! But know your heart is pure and you are made of pure light. For this reason, you will always be stronger. Now follow my lead!

<Watch behind you! Don't let them sneak up on you! You can sense, feel, and see everything around you. Use it to your advantage. Feel them coming before they move! Good job, Kheira. You are moving like your old self!>

—*Breathe, focus, calm my thoughts, and anticipate his moves! I see it now! He is very agile, and a fierce opponent, but all of his actions are fueled by anger. He can't sense the life force all around him! Stillness is what is required! I call on the forces of the elementals and the power of water! Help me defeat my enemy and protect what we hold sacred! If I bend the wind just right, and call on my Divine Mother, Yemeya, to help me wield the power of the ocean. I can blow this entire army backward and drown them in the ocean. Let me steady myself. My staff holds power on its own, I'll spin it in a circle till the fierce force of the wind is directed in their direction. Great, it is working now. I'll let go of the staff. Step backward and use the powers my Divine Mother has gifted me with, to unleash the fierceness of the ocean upon them.*

—Kheira, that was amazing! Watching you use your unique combat style, your powers to harness nature; and you remembered your connection to your Divine Mother! My Light, I see the memories returning in your eyes! You are so elegant and graceful! There has been no one like you before and there never will be again, I am so proud of you, My Light. Now that you have single-handedly defeated the army, we must leave! Urgently! Wrap your heart's light around me and I'll wrap mine around you. We will head immediately to Planet Moriahn until we can ensure our passage home is safe.

—I don't understand. Why would we need to ensure it is safe before going back to our home?

—I will explain all, in due time, My Light! I see you are now ready for complete transparency. I will fill you in on all the missing pieces, my word always remains true!

—Lovely, that is the last thing I remember. Khogee promised me full disclosure once we got to Planet Moriahn, but the next thing I remember is us being here on Planet Saynohs. I don't know how we ended up here instead of Moriahn or how we got separated. I just know somehow Khogee has also lost the memory of who he is as well. I've lived hundreds, possibly thousands, of lives on this planet. All in an effort to find him so we can go home. In the lives I've been successful in finding him, I am successful in helping him partially awake only some of the time. But, I am never successful in helping him remember the fullness of who he is. I've yet to locate him in this incarnation and I'm starting to give into the negative thoughts. I feel all hope is lost. In previous incarnations where I'm successful in finding him, I do so when I awaken on the astral plane. Then I'm able to locate him in this perverted form of reality and be whatever he needs. All in an effort to help him remember his own soul's connection, in order for him to trace himself back to his spirit. But, no matter how hard I have tried, Lovely, I haven't been able to locate him on the astral plane. What am I doing wrong?

—You must know what you seek is the connection back to his light. I think you've forgotten this important link when you have been searching for him. In all the incarnations you've had with each other on this planet you are always each other's opposites in form, right? I believe you have started to associate the connection between the two of you with the forms you have been incarnating in. You are magnets with opposite charges always pulling your light back together. I hope our exercise this morning, with you recalling your time on Kaytoin, has allowed you to once again remember how his light feels. Allow the light of his soul to draw you to him. Instead of you relying on what you see with your eyes, rely on what you feel in your heart. I promise you he is here in this incarnation. The only way for you to locate him is for you to start searching for him with the light deep in your soul.

Chapter 3:

I Need You

—I am really hungry. I sure hope the vegetarian spot around the corner is open! I've never been by on a Sunday and I'm not sure of the hours. Ahhh, I see lights. Do I dare say I see a person or two inside? Yes, Yes, I do. So, glad they are open. I really don't feel like cooking today. Hmmm, I wonder if Mama G is hungry as well. I'll pick her up something just in case. Who is this woman behind the register? I've never seen her before.

—Hi, may I take your order?

—Yes, I'd like two taco bowls.

—What would you like for your grain?

—Quinoa.

—Hmmm, something seems really off.

—And your protein?

—Black Beans.

—What is so off about her? Now that I look, this entire staff is different from the usual people I see. And there is no one else here but me. This place is usually jumping. Best vegetarian food around! Okay, maybe I am being paranoid, someone else just came in.

—Kheira, I need you. Find me and help me remember.

—Why am I hearing Khogee call out to me? I don't understand!

—Number 9 your order is ready.

—Thank you. When did you all stop bringing the food out to the table?

—Oh, it is a new policy of ours.

—Okay, thanks again. I guess I'll sit over here. Oh, excuse me, ma'am. I didn't see you standing there. Here let me pick your keys up for you. Sorry, for knocking them out of your hand.

—Thanks, but I'm not old enough to be a ma'am. My name is Kheira.

—It's nice to meet you. My name is Kho.

—Khogee, is that you?

—Sorry, I'm not Khogee but, wait, I do recognize you. I see you at night in my dreams on a regular basis. You are the woman…

—Kheira, baby, it is time to get up.

—No, Mama G, you just woke me up from a lucid dream. I believe I was seeing, never mind! I'm up, Mama G. I'll be there shortly.

—Lovely, Lovely, Lovely… Are you there? I found him; it is the first time I've seen him in a dream in this incarnation. He recognized me from his dreams, but he doesn't know me. Actually, the entire dream was very strange. The people working at the restaurant where I saw him were all implants, I've never seen any of these staff members before. Also, I heard him call out to me telepathically before I bumped into him in my dream, but then when I bumped into him, he didn't know me. Which doesn't make any sense. I know it was a premonition, but something just seemed so different and off. What is your take, Lovely?

—Guard this information with your life. Don't let anyone know about this dream. You must not trust anyone.

—What about Mama G? I can surely confide in her though, right?

—TRUST NO ONE! I cannot emphasize enough the importance of you keeping any and all information regarding Khogee to yourself. In the dream you stated everyone working at the restaurant, you have never seen before. Correct?

—Yes, this is correct.

—And that you heard him speak to you telepathically right before you bumped into him.

—Yes. Lovely, this is also correct. What does all this mean?

—My best guess is that the dream was an implant. They must know you are here.

—Who knows we are here?

—The agents. The agents who have been tracking you and Khogee down through time to end both of your existences.

—Kheira, sweetie. What was that you said? I couldn't make it out.

—Oh, Mama G, it was nothing. I'm here at your disposal. How may I assist you?

—Sweetie, do you mind going down there to the Grain House, and getting me a taco bowl? I want quinoa, black beans, and extra taco seasoning. Tell them to pack the veggies in there, as many as will fit. Don't forget my guac, sour cream, pico, and salsa on the side.

—Okay, Mama G! Let me throw on some clothes. I do have to run uptown first so it may take a little longer than usual.

—Okay, baby, I'm not going anywhere. But, don't forget I'm hungry.

—Lovely, are you still there?

—Always!

—Why did you say I can't tell Mama G about the recording? And what did you mean about the agents implanting my dream?

—You haven't remembered everything from the last planet you were on with Khogee. What else do you remember?

—Other than all the billions of incarnations I've spent here in an effort to reconnect with Khogee? Absolutely nothing.

—Billions? Exaggerations will not help you, neither will feeling sorry for yourself. Focus, and stay diligent. I know you think you remember all your incarnations here, but you don't. You also don't remember what happened on your home planet that caused you and Khogee to leave so urgently, deserting all of your family and friends. Remember the truth in its totality and then you will know who to trust.

—Wait, what about Khogee? Can I not trust him?

—You strengthen each other's light. You and he are the light that makes each other's light shine brighter. You are one and the same and will always be able to trust one another. The light you share is powerful and of the most unique kind.

—What is so unique about the light we share, Lovely?

—Now you are asking the correct questions, Kheira. However, I have already said too much, and cannot say anymore on the matter. I must go. Before I do, please remember, when you find Khogee, stand in front of him eye to eye. Allow your souls to greet and your hearts to speak to each other before words ever leave your lips. He will help you find the connection back to who you are, and all the moments in time you have lost. For him, you will do the same. Know that together you are both unstoppable. Never forget I'm only a thought away. I will always be here when you need me.

—Wait, Lovely. I feel you know more than you are telling me. Why do you hold back?

—That is not my role. I can only guide you, ensure you and Khogee's mission does not fail. I cannot impede on your free will. Therefore I am not able to say or reveal all that I know. As my role is not to control the outcome, only guide you through your decisions and thoughts to help you stay on the path.

Chapter 4:

Trust

—Grain House! Am I sure I want to stop and get food from the same place I saw Khogee last night in my dreams? Especially when Lovely warned me that the dream could have been an implant from agents? I got this. Stay out of my head, take a deep breath, focus my mind, and stay in this moment. I'm going to walk slowly and observe everything! I need to control my expectations. That dream could just be letting me know he is nearby, not an actual premonition that he is here or harm is on the horizon. Besides, in all my past incarnations that I am able to recall, I always dream of him at a place where I am. Whether it be the lake, mountains, or ocean, I end up at that same location the next day and he is never there. Maybe I'm actually remembering moments from past lives or I'm tapped into alternate timelines. Or possibly that dream was a manifestation of my desires and there are no agents or Khogee inside. In past lifetimes, after a dream sighting of Khogee, it is always weeks or months later before our paths actually cross. From what I've gathered, the dream is the first stage of the process. It's like an alarm going off to let me know our connection, our light, is drawing us closer.

—Let's focus. We can do this, Kheira. Simply open the door and walk in. Khogee is not going to be here. Let's just get our food and go!

—Whew! See, look. I knew I could do it. I made it inside. See, he is nowhere to be found. Hmm, but just like the dream I had last night, something is off! This is different, everything in here looks the exact same as it did in my dream. That is very unusual. When I come to a place I dreamed about the night before, there are ALWAYS differences! The layout of the place, the colors, the people, or the animals are always different, but this is exactly how I dreamed it. Even down to the entirely new staff I have never seen. Maybe Lovely was right, maybe the dream was an implant by agents. I need to stay alert and on guard! Or should I just leave? No, I can't, if this is a chance for me to reconnect with Khogee, I must stay! Wow, even the lady at the register is the same woman from my dream. I expected there to be a man, not a woman. Either way, I still do not recognize her, she has never been at the counter anytime I have come.

—Hi, my name is Callie. I'll be your food practitioner today. What can I order for you?

—*Let's see what happens if I change some things from the dream like my order.*

—Yes, Callie, I'd like two grain bowls.

—Wonderful, what is your seasoning?

—Taco for the first bowl. Mediterranean, garlic, and herb for the second bowl. Please, add extra veggies to both of them and quinoa as the grain.

—Your protein?

—Lentils please.

—Any drinks?

—No, that will be all, thank you.

—You are welcome, your total will be $25.25.

—Hmm, have the prices changed?

—No, they are the same as usual. I've been here a year and that is the usual price for two grain bowls.

—*Okay, I know something is wrong. She is lying, these aren't the prices. Let's see where this goes.*

—A year you say, do you usually work on the morning shift during the weekdays?

—Oh no, I always work the afternoon and evening shifts right here at the register. Your number is fifty-two, I'll call your number when your order is ready.

—Thank you, Callie.

—When did they get order numbers? These are definitely agents and whatever they tried to implant in my brain via the dream last night didn't work. They changed this entire construct. I will not ask any more questions. I don't want to tip them off and help them realize the implant didn't work. Hopefully, they haven't already figured out that I'm not under their hypnosis in this simulation. I need to sit down and gather my thoughts. This is a new scenario for me. Who are these agents? And, why are they here tracking me and Khogee down? I must figure out how we both can remember.

—Excuse me, did you drop your number?

—Who is this talking to me now? I really need to focus on a plan.

—I'm sorry, ma'am. Did you drop your number?

—Thank you, I must have not realized that I…

—Wait! Is that really Khogee?

—Her essence is so familiar. Her scent I know. Wait! It is her. The girl I've been seeing in my dreams at night for the past month! How can this be! I'm so confused right now.

—I'm Khogee, it is nice to meet you. I apologize for startling you, but you dropped this, your order number.

—It's okay, thank you for picking it up. I'm Kheira. It is nice to meet you. Thank you, I was so lost in my thoughts, I didn't realize I'd dropped it.

—No problem. And, I am sorry for staring at you so intensely, but I feel as though we know each other, yet I don't remember ever meeting you. Are you here alone?

—Yes. Do you mind if I join you for lunch/dinner, Kheira? No, not at all. I know this may sound crazy but…

—NO! You can't just tell this girl you've been dreaming of her for weeks and that you've fallen in love with her. That's crazy talk and she'll run right out of here. Tact, we need tact. Let's slow down and go with the flow.

<No, I will not run. That will only slow down our mission!>

— <Wait! What! How did you…? Are you able to communicate with me telepathically?>

— <Yes, it is one of the best ways to communicate! But you don't seem as alarmed or shocked for someone having a telepathic conversation for the first time, that they remember. Why is that?>

—Well, since you heard what I was thinking you know I've been dreaming of you for weeks on end.

In those dreams, we are always speaking telepathically. It's as if my soul has been getting me prepared for this moment.

—Khogee, something is off I don't quite understand! You never recognize me! You never know who I am!

—What do you mean?

—Well, you are my soul's true mate. We amplify each other's light and bring out the best in one another! We have been reincarnating on this planet for centuries, with one goal in mind. For me to wake you up from your slumber so you can remember who you are. And, in turn, help me to remember the fullness of who I am, so we can go home! But every time I find you, you never remember immediately, never wake up right away! How is this possible now? That you've been dreaming of moments we have shared throughout time, before we even came to this planet?

—Excuse me, number fifty-two your order is ready.

—Thank you!

—Do you need anything else?

—No, this is perfect.

—*Hmm, I saw her look directly at the order number, I wonder why she didn't take it.*

—Let's eat, my love. We can talk more telepathically as we eat.

—*He called me "my love." The Khogee I know has never used the phrase "my love" when speaking to me.*

—Here, Kheira, you look distracted. Let me feed you!

— <KHEIRA, WAIT! Don't eat any of the food, it is poisoned.>

— <What in the world is going on? Who is this speaking to me in my sacred heart space?>

— <It's me.>

— <Khogee? Huh, well then why are you telling me not to eat, while you are trying to feed me at the same time?>

— <My Light, he is a clone, an imposter out to harm you. I need you to trust me and come meet me in the bathroom immediately.>

— <Well, if you are talking to me in my sacred heart space, will he not hear you and know the plan? He is connected to me and hears my thoughts.>

— <No! He is not and does not. Because he is not real, only a fake copy of that which is real. He can only tap into what is in your mind space, but he has no soul. So, he will never be able to truly connect with yours! You see, the agent from behind the counter left the order ticket number fifty-two when she brought you your food. It has a transmitter in it that allows him to connect to your mind's space. I heard your thoughts when you noticed she didn't take the number after she brought you your food, now you know why.

I know this is a very confusing situation but I need you to connect your heart with mine, look deep into my soul and focus! Remember your training! Tune into his heart, into the essence of who he is. Do you see or feel any light? Now focus on me, on my heart! Tune everything out and tell me do you feel and sense, My Light? Do you feel the connection to your own light with me or with him? Now, Kheira, tell me what it is your soul already knows.>

— <It's you, the light that makes My Light shine brighter. I feel nothing from him. He is empty, a pit of perpetual darkness rotating in and out of itself.>

— <Now, I need you to be quick. We must not waste time, excuse yourself from the table and come to the bathroom while we devise an exit strategy.>

—Kheira, my love, where'd you go? Seemed as though you completely spaced out.

—Sorry, I have so much on my mind. Excuse me for a moment, I need to use the lady's room.

—Sure, but you really should take a bite of your food before you leave. You know, to make sure it is up to your standards.

—Oh, it's fine, I'm sure it tastes as yummy as it always does. I'll be back shortly!

—Khogee, it is really you!

—Yes, My Light, it is me. Come and embrace me.

—I don't understand what's going on here, none of this makes any sense.

—I know you are confused. This isn't how our past lives have gone here on this planet. But I promise in time I'll explain everything.

—Forgive me if I am not too confident in you right now. Last time I heard 'I'll explain everything' we ended up on Saynohs lost in a cycle of reincarnations for hundreds of years. And how exactly do you all of a sudden have remembrance of how our past lives have gone on this planet?

—My Light, do you no longer trust me?

—You know I do, with every fiber of my being.

—Then know I would have never separated from you by my own will. Someone trapped us here and erased our memories. They tried to break our connection, but our link originates from our light, not our minds! They felt they succeeded, but our connection can never be broken! Someone came to me and made me aware of what was going on here in your reality. I know you remember almost everything about this planet and the awakening that began for you on Kaytoin, but you still don't remember beyond this, correct?

—Yes, that is correct. Now, can you tell me who this person is that awakened you?

—In time, My Light, we can discuss all. For now, let us focus on our exit strategy.

—*WOW, I'm always amazed, no matter how much time passes before we reconnect, Khogee always makes me feel like a thousand suns rising to shine a light on all that's dark.*

—My Light, know and feel deep within your essence my love for you. Let it guide you and strengthen you as we fight our way out of here.

—Fight? Why must we fight? Can't we just walk out?

—No, we cannot! Someone changed the codes here! Look there are no longer windows in this bathroom! Wait, how'd you know there were windows in this bathroom? I eat at this chain on a regular basis. I now know you do as well.

Listen, My Light, our light's connection will never be unbound. No matter where we are, or how far apart we are physically, our souls will always seek each other out. I know you have lots of questions, but first, we must escape this restaurant and figure out our next steps. I have a secret hideout, let's get there, we can catch up and proceed forward with understanding what steps we need to take to continue forward with our mission! For now, let's focus on a way out because the layout of this place has been changed completely. There is now only one way in and one way out.

—How do you figure?

—I saw an exit right before I turned the corner to come toward the bathroom. There are also windows all around the restaurant. We can break one and make a quick exit if needed. Kheira, I know what you see with your physical eyes, but close them and use your first eye to see. Now, tell me again what you think you saw.

—Oh, my goodness I see it now, there is code everywhere creating an illusion. There are no windows nor a real door under the exit sign. Some kind of program is being run to feed images that look like outside, but there is really nothing but brick walls everywhere except the front door. Why do you think someone would go through this much trouble to capture us? I know we have spoken before about them wanting to kill us, but if that was the case, whoever they are could have done that instead of trapping us in a simulated reality. Where everyone is asleep and does not even realize it. There has to be more going on here.

—Yes, My Light, I agree, and we will discuss it all once we…

—I know, I know, once we fight our way out of here and make it to your secret lair.

—Don't be like that. My Light, I need you to concentrate and connect with my heart. We will create a forcefield of protection around us like we did when we were headed for Planet Moriahn.

—How do you remember what happened on Kaytoin?

—Focus, Kheira. Know you are protected and take this!

—My Staff! How'd you?

—No more questions, My Light. Focus and remember like water we move together, always fluid and in sync. Silence your mind, feel my heart, allow our connection to flow! Do you feel my heart space?

—Yes, I do!

—Great. Know you are always connected to my soul. Feel the life force flowing through your body. Feel the life force moving around and through you. Connect with your staff and don't fight against the flow. Remember these are level three agents. They move stealthily and are trained in several combat styles. Don't underestimate them! Know who you are and don't second guess yourself. Allow your life force to guide you. On three, we move. One, two, three.

— <Watch your six. Two agents are flanking you!>

— <I see them through your eyes, Kheira. I am your eyes and you are mine.>

—I hear three agents moving around me, I feel their moves before they make them. My staff is unbreakable, and I am swift and mighty. As I move like the water, I gain momentum and flexibility. Agent one is slow on the instep, two jabs to his lower right torso and a quick break to his right arm should dismantle him. Wow, that was quicker than I thought. I took all three agents out without a sweat. With Khogee saying these are level three agents, I figured this fight would be more challenging.

—My Light, I saw you. You moved like flowing water, such grace and poise; no matter how hard you try to escape, the water will overtake you with ease.

—Me? You moved so swiftly like a roaring wind that you can never see, just feel as it thrashes you to the ground. But, that battle was so easy! It was too easy! You said they were level three agents. I'm not sure exactly what that means, but the way you described their level of skill, knowing multiple combat styles. The fight shouldn't have been that easy.

—I agree, My Light. Something is off. I am just not sure what. Those hunting us have agents and the group they call the assassins. We met the assassins on our exit from Kaytoin, the planet we left before we landed here on Saynohs. Agents have five levels, one through five. Five being the most lethal. With these agents being level three, this fight should have been more of a challenge. Agents are trained in an indoor facility by machines, and as a result, they are more predictable. They are fierce, and typically lack fluidity and the natural ability of improvisation. Their moves are more calculated, stiff, and at times telegraphed.

—Is that why it felt like time slowed down, when I was fighting them, and I knew their moves before they made them, because they were telegraphing?

—Partially, but mainly because you are tapping into your gifts. We are way more advanced than the coding in this reality and therefore can move in and out of time. Your soul remembers how, but that organic computer in the head of the body you currently occupy doesn't. The assassins on the other hand only have one level, pure evil! They are a creation of those hunting us infused with pure hate and a thirst for blood. You see the agents have a soul, but through programming, they have been put under the hypnosis of delusion. Whereas those creatures we fought on Kaytoin have no soul at all.

—What about us? What kind of fighters are we?

—We are warriors, and we have three levels. For us, level one is the most lethal! We train from the time we can start walking. We are trained by those who come before us. Our level-one warriors have an even greater advantage. The gods of nature and the elementals bestow us with the blessing of being able to harness nature's power. You will also find that our divine parents have also blessed us with power and gifts as well. I don't think any more agents are coming but either way we can't stay here. We must go. Let's go outside to see if you remember the last ability we were working on, before we had our memories wiped, again.

—It is so strange how you remembered nothing for lifetimes, but now once again you remember everything, and are teaching me the truth. I don't understand how your memories were put back online but mine have not been.

—Come, don't fret, My Light. Place your body against mine, close your eyes, and feel my heartbeat. Feel the energy between us, slowly feel the energy wrap itself around us. Now breathe.

—I love this gift, look we are floating in the air again. Hopefully invisible to all in this reality.

—So, you do remember the last lesson we worked on.

—Yes, I also remember the last battle we had before we ended up here, lost in a cycle of incarnations. I also remember you leaving a piece of yourself back on that planet to fight while the rest of you and I escaped.

—I had to protect you. I know you don't understand all, but you will. We are powerful beings. Our abilities go beyond your wildest imagination. And when properly balanced and aligned we can create worlds if we choose.

—There is just so much for me to learn.

—No, My Light, you need only remember. When you do, all will make sense. Now let's get to safety and figure out our next move. If agents have been sent after us, we are no longer safe here.

—It is so amazing up here. Floating above the ground. The higher we go the smaller and more insignificant everything below seems.

—Yes, I agree. When we are flying up above all that is below, so much is put into perspective, allowing you to question how one can get so caught up in the distractions. Then once you descend you forget all that you saw and perceived when you were at that higher state. It is the descent that gets you, because once you land you get lost in the everyday hustle and bustle completely forgetting how small and insignificant everything is in the bigger scheme of things.

—You are sure no one can see us floating above them?

—Yes, I am sure they cannot see us. We are invisible. Once we come together, connect, and create our outer protection bubble we have the ability to use this shield to make ourselves invisible if we desire. Besides, most people go all day without ever looking up; so even if we weren't invisible to the naked eye, I doubt anyone would notice us.

—You know I also remember you materializing in my room out of nowhere, right?

—I'd never assume you'd forget such a thing.

—If we can, assuming I have this ability as well, materialize wherever we want, why exactly are we floating to our next destination? Why did we have to float off the last planet versus just materializing back home?

—Do you not enjoy being close to me and spending time with me? Does my breath stink or something?

—Stop being lip-smart and just answer the question.

—Truthfully, I enjoy spending time with you, this gives us a chance to connect and be close. However, we can materialize wherever we want inside the confines of the code we are currently interacting with. For whatever reason, since we have been gone from our home planet, we have forgotten the ability to walk through time from one system of codes to another.

—So, what is next? We can't float around up here forever! If agents know we are here, can we be safe? But what is the point in going anywhere else, and why send agents this time when they sent the assassins last time? I have so many questions! We are moving from planet to planet, but they keep tracking us down. How? We are missing something! My guide, Lovely, has informed me to trust no one except you and her. I'm still searching to figure out the true depths of this message!

—I agree, something is not right. We have missed something and need to regroup. Let's speed this up and head to my hideout.

—You aren't thinking of leaving the same way we left the other planet are you, we know how that ended!

—Who is being lip smart now? Come closer, look into my eyes.

—Yeah, I know, feel you, and trust you.

—Trust me, you haven't even begun to feel me, My Light! I promise you that.

—Wow! Your secret hideout is quite nice!

—Thank you, My Light.

—Now, tell me, what was that I heard on the journey here? It was a quiet whisper hidden in the back of your mind. Hmm, was it 'I need you more than you know!' Then I heard a faint scream.

—Oh, you were searching my heart and mind, huh? You heard whispers of my heart. Memories and thoughts from times long ago! Connections to you. Connections you can tap into whenever we connect. That particular memory was from an ancient time when we were young. We were practicing our abilities unsupervised. You decided to teleport without me and ended up in a Lava pit on Planet Ninotah! I felt your fear and connected with your energy. When I saw you in my first eye, I connected with your heart and told you I would come to you. You told me no, as you knew it would be a no return trip. I ignored your request for me to stay. I teleported to you just as you lost hold of your float; we both were being consumed by the lava pit. The scream you heard was us being consumed by the lava pit. We embraced one another, I told you I will never leave you as our connection, our bond is beyond infinite.

—WOW! I actually remember that event. Your very last words to me were, until next time My Light, feel me in your soul!

—Yes, My Light, now you are starting to remember just how deep our roots go!

—The remembrance of that event and how we always regenerated with full awareness of our previous lives makes me feel so sorry for all the inhabitants of this planet. I don't understand why the people of this planet reincarnate without their full memories, or at least partial memories that will help them evolve and grow so they can transcend whatever this place is. Why are they wiped clean? Who is responsible for playing this horrible trick on these people? It is almost like they are an experiment. To constantly live full lives, be removed from the game by what they believe is an event called death, just to be put back in the game as a new character with no memories! I don't understand. How will the people of this planet ever know the truth of who they are, and what they can become? I don't know how much longer I can knowingly keep doing this dog and pony show over and over again.

—I know, My Light, we have to figure out how to get out of here. Let's get rest for now and discuss more when we awake. I just know there is something we are missing.

Chapter 5:

You're Never Alone

—Khogee, what's going on? Why are you leaving?

—My Light, I was hoping to be gone before you woke, to prevent the pain of having to see me depart.

—What do you mean, depart? I thought we were going to figure out a plan together?

—I couldn't tell you the truth yesterday. You were so happy to see me.

—You aren't making sense. Speak to me plainly and clearly, what is going on?

—My Light, I am not from this timeline. I left you a note right there by your shoes to explain everything. I couldn't bear to look you in your eyes! You see, I'm Khogee, but I'm not the Khogee from this timeline. I am from another timeline. We came up with a plan to save you from the ambush that would have taken you back through another cycle of being wiped and birthed back into unknowingness. We don't have time for that to happen! It is now or never—freedom must be ours! Kheira, I know this is all so confusing. Speak to me, My Light, what questions do you have? I am listening.

—Who is 'we'?

—We are and always will be you and I.

—Please, explain to me sincerely and deeply as I do not understand. How did you know about the event with the lava pit if you are not my Khogee?

—Well, while I'm here I'm able to have complete symbiosis with him. In other words, I can tap into his thoughts, even the ones he himself does not remember.

My Light, it was never my intention to cause you pain. I feel you in my heart right now and see the confusion on your face. Here, let's do this. First, give me your hands, close your eyes, concentrate, and align your heart with mine. Breathe gently and allow me to show you as I explain.

It started last Wednesday. I was in my armor room cleaning my blades, preparing for a sparring session with my good friend Antonne. When a huge portal opened before my eyes. There was nothing but pure light for a second then I saw vegetation of a kind I've never seen before, colors so vibrant it made me want to cry! Then a long thick chocolate leg stepped through. To my amazement, it was you. You were clothed in gold battle armor and had blood on your spear. I was completely caught off guard by your radiance, and fell to my knees. As your skin literally glowed with a gold light all over. You looked into my soul deeply, then connected with my heart space advising me to stand up! I immediately rushed to my mini fridge and got you water, as I could tell you'd been in a long battle. You then took the water and used some of it to create a chair for you and me to sit on.

Then you explained to me that you and I have been the most successful on her timeline, and we were on the last leg of our mission. Had we succeeded in winning this particular battle all would've been set right and we would have won the war. In other words, we would be free. Well, something went wrong. Someone betrayed us! The 'me' from that timeline sacrificed himself to save the 'you' of that timeline. She was being flanked from four sides, and by the time she realized it a spear was a couple of inches from her heart. The 'me' there teleported in front of her to save her. She advised that as a result the mission could not be completed, because the only way the mission can be completed is if we do it together. She could read that I was confused and didn't quite understand why she was there in that moment talking to me. What was her purpose of seeking me out? Why was she telling me all this? She read my heart and understood my concern. She advised me that I must come to this timeline to save you. The mission has failed on all other timelines but this one, and this has never happened before. In other words, your timeline is the only timeline where both of us are still walking around.

Which helped her to see the betrayal was far deeper than she had realized. So, today, had she not sent me, you would have been next.

—I don't understand. I have so many questions. If you aren't my Khogee, then where is he? And can you tell me what happened to the 'me' on your timeline?

—Well, you were never born.

—What do you mean I was never born? We always come in together.

—On my timeline, I have seen you in my dreams while I'm asleep. And when I am awake, I see you in my visions. I've felt such a deep connection to you and never understood why. What the you that came to me informed me when I told her that I'd dreamed of her; is that the you on my timeline was never born because your mother was tricked into ending your life before it began. As far as your Khogee on this timeline. I left details in the note. He has not awoken and is lost in the delusions of this illusion. You must find him and help him to remember who he is.

—How do I find him?

—*I feel crushed! I thought we had come back together, just to find out again I'm on my own!*

—I feel how hurt you are, but trust me you will succeed! And know deep in your soul, My Light, that you are never alone! Relax, breathe, and feel him! The connection you all have is always present, the link can never be broken. All you have to do is feel it. And, no matter what happens, don't give up. I don't care how hard the journey ahead gets. Don't give up on yourself or Khogee! I promise the two of you are very close in the vicinity. You will find him, trust me.

— <Khogee, it's time for you to leave.>

—Kheira, sorry, My Light, but the other you is calling me back I must leave you now.

—Yes, I see the portal right behind you, and you weren't lying about the light. It is so pure it's almost blinding. But, I don't want you to leave. I feel as if I could just come with you and we finish our mission on your timeline. However, I know I would never have any peace with that choice! Knowingly leaving my Khogee behind to fend for himself!

—Kheira, My Light, I'm glad your love for Khogee supersedes your need for comfort. He needs your light Kheira, to help him find his way out of the darkness.

—Khogee, you must come now, you can't stay here any longer. You can't be gone too long or those who watch your life streams across the timelines will notice. You must come back to your home to fulfill your purpose here. Know that when the time has come you all will be one!

Kheira, raise up your head and look me in my eyes. Know yourself and remember who you truly are. You are strong with immeasurable powers beyond your wildest dreams. Accept who you are and accept your power. Stop fighting the awakening happening in you and embrace who you are!!

—How do you know so much!

—I am you, Kheira, and I know myself, therefore I know you. I am you and you are me! The timelines are all merging. Therefore, what was separate is now one. I now come from what will be your future and I have been traveling through all the possibilities helping to even the score. As they are traveling backward to change what is! Not knowing they will never succeed in their dark agenda! That is how I know you will! Your Khogee is over by Ninth and First Streets, the northeast corner. Find him, feel his soul and remember your bond, remember your connection. Help him to see through the illusion to the truth, the way he has done for you in ancient times. Feel the foundation of trust that your bond is built on, know your bond transcends time, this reality, and dimensions. It will never be broken. Kheira we must go, but I need you to remember some things. You and Khogee always surrender to each other, there is never a power struggle between the two of you. Understand?

—Yes, I understand.

—Secondly, there will come a point in time where he tells you to heed his warning, and not proceed on your attended course of action without him by your side. In this moment you will feel his soul and understand his urgency, make sure you do not proceed on your attended course of action without him. When he says wait, you kneel! This simple action will save you from great loss!

—How will I know when that moment arises?

—Trust yourself Kheira, your soul will guide you. My words will rise from the depths of your heart like a faint echo in the distance, and there will be no doubt or question in you, you must surrender! Lastly, I need you to know that I'm only a thought away. Just think Lovely, and I'll be here to guide you in any way you need.

—Wait! Lovely? That is you?

Chapter 6:

The Key

—Ninth and First Street. I'm here, but all I see is a bunch of houses. Hmmm, well, that is different, all three of these two-story houses share the same gate. Okay, I see a sign on the middle gate. Here we go, Kheira; I feel this is the place. But what would Khogee be doing at 'The School of Lord Thoth?' Proceed forward we must!

—Hello, dear. I hope you are having a wonderful day! Please, come in, are you here to apply for the open assistant position? Our founder is currently leading a session. You are welcome to join. As soon as he is done, he'll have a few words with you. Sorry, I'm rambling, I didn't even introduce myself. I'm Suzette, I'm the lead house attendee for the House of Sekhmet. This is Ronald. He is the lead house attendee for the House of Anpu. The boys sleep and live there, and of course, the girls stay in the Sekhmet House. See, if you look just over there to your left you can see the Sekhmet House, right there through that window. Currently, we have twenty-six kids staying with us. They are all thirteen through eighteen years of age. We do our best to keep an equal number of girls and boys, we find it keeps more balance in the home. Right now, we have an equal number of both genders. In each house we separate the younger age group from the older group, keeping the thirteen- to fifteen-year-olds sleeping quarters separate from the sixteen- to eighteen-year-old group. Through the night we also keep a chaperone right by the entrance of the door for each group, to ensure the safety of all children. We complete heavy background checks of these chaperones and the security guards to ensure the safety of all. Okay, dear, here we go. We've arrived at the Great Hall of Solace.

—Wow, it's actually him, he is breathtaking. Deep caramel chocolate skin that matches my own. He even has my hazel brown eyes. My goodness, those broad shoulders and biceps. I'm going to need to do some deep breathing to get centered and stay focused. My, how I have missed him. I wonder if he will even recognize me.

—I'm sorry, dear, I forgot to get your name.

—Oh, yes, Suzette. I'm Kheira. It's a pleasure to meet you.

—Dear, I've always loved that name but regrettably don't personally know anyone with that name. I just remember a lady checking me out at the store and I couldn't pronounce the name on her name tag. When she advised me it's pronounced Khe-ruh, I thought to myself, now that is such a beautiful name. Why aren't there more Kheiras in my small slice of the world? Oh, Khogee, you didn't end early on account of us, did you? She is here about the assistant position.; I was showing her around, we can come back later.

—No, it is perfectly fine. We actually wrapped early, no fuss. Thank you so much, Suzette! I know you are super busy. I'll take over the tour from here.

—No, I couldn't interrupt your busy day, I was just bringing her by for a few words with you. I know how busy your days always are, plus you have a meeting with Bob's Food Supply in an hour. So, I'll finish…

—Thank you so much for your eagerness to assist. I will finish the tour with Kheira, we really need to fill that assistant position ASAP. Can you please clear my calendar for the rest of the day? Reschedule all of the meetings you can for tomorrow please.

—And if they aren't available tomorrow? I must insist you meet with Bob today. We must have our supplies!

—You are correct, that is a meeting that must happen. Can you and Ronald meet with Bob on my behalf, please?

—If you insist. I'll get Ronald and we will get on top of that right away.

—I'm sorry about that, Kheira. If you come this way we can converse privately.

—Wait, I've noticed this is the second time you have called me by my name. How exactly do you know to call me Kheira—Suzette never formally introduced us.

—You are so exquisite! And, you've grown your hair all the way out.

—Excuse me, Khogee? Do you know me?

—Well, yes and no! Come with me to my office so we can talk discreetly. It is right over here. Sorry, I didn't mean to grab your hand. It's just... come into my office—I'll explain in more detail.

Kheira, I've dreamed of you for the last few years. I thought at first it was just a weird dream. But the dreams kept happening, increasing in frequency every year. Some dreams seem to be a continuation of one another while other dreams I have consistently.

—Can you give me an example of one of the dreams you have had repeatedly?

—Sure, there is one dream I have a lot, I'd say the most. You and I are fighting these very ugly creatures. However, how ugly they are is not the strangest part. The strangest part is that we are fighting them in the sky. Keep in mind we don't have jet boots, we aren't on hoverboards, or inside of a flying robot. I mean you and I are literally flying, without any kind of wings, may I add. We are flying and annihilating these creatures. I never stop being amazed at seeing you harness the power of the wind and ocean to defeat the entire army approaching us. Then we fly to each other, press our bodies into one another. Some kind of dome of light forms around us, and we just fly away. Then I always randomly wake up at the part where we are flying away, and never get to see what happens next. So, not only do I keep having the same dream, but as I'm telling you this, I'm realizing I have it at the same time every day right before I wake. I've never repeated this to anyone. I'm sure I sound crazy right about now. I mean I feel a tad bit crazy saying it out loud. And by the look on your face, I know you think I'm crazy. I should have never said anything!

—Wow!

—Seriously, are you laughing at me? In a moment of complete vulnerability, I tell you a very intimate detail about my life—a detail I haven't shared with anyone—and your response is to laugh at me? Can you please share with me what is so funny to you?

—You. You are funny! However, my intention is not to make you feel insecure, My Light. I apologize if that is the feeling my actions produced. It is just that I have never seen you like this before and I mean never. You are always so poised, in control, calm, and so confident! Never out of sorts! You are always together, even in the face of death. And, I can't help but think if this is how I sounded to you when the roles were reversed. When I was the one buried under the weight of pain, unable to remember who I was. Please forgive me, My Light.

—Thank you for clarifying. It really helps ease how insecure I was feeling in the moment. However, I still feel a bit off-kilter, you know, like a mental patient.

—Let's try some deep breathing to see if it helps ground you more. Take my hands, look me in my eyes, and watch me. I'm going to breathe deeply through my nose and circulate the air directly into my stomach. Then I am going to hold my breath for five seconds. At the end of the five seconds, I am going to breathe out very slowly through my mouth for another count of five. Okay, now you do it with me. Breathe in. Hold, one, two, three, four, five. Great now breathe out. Great job. Now, let's do it two more times. How do you feel?

—I feel calmer and more present, thank you. Now can you please tell me…?

—No, I cannot! No, more talking from you for a few minutes. Okay? Just listen to me for a bit, okay?

—My Light, I need you to understand that what you are seeing isn't a dream. It is a memory your soul is playing back to you, to help you remember who you are. In past lifetimes on this planet when I found you, you have never dreamed of me, nor have you ever remembered me. Normally, my light is needed to jump-start your awakening, but it's as if your soul has been attempting to wake you up on its own. I may have underestimated just how important our mission is this time around. Does any of this make sense to you?

—Oh. So I have permission to talk now? If so, let me start off by saying, it is going to take a moment for my brain to comprehend and process your words. However, deep in my heart, I feel relief, as my soul recognizes the truth in your words. If it is okay with you, I'd like to explore other dreams I've had. But before we go down that rabbit hole, I need to better understand what you meant by the statement 'You have never seen me like this before.'

—This is going to be a lot of information. I'm not sure if your consciousness is at a place where you are ready to receive the wattage.

—Try me!

—So, you think you can handle this? Well, time is currently not on our side. You know what, let's do it. Come from behind your desk and sit in the chair beside me. Wait, first let's turn the chairs where they are facing one another, and let's put them close enough where our legs support one another. Before we start, please make sure that door is locked.

—Make sure the door is locked? You aren't really here to kidnap me, are you?

—My Light, I couldn't kidnap you if I tried. Now make haste and lock the door, please. I don't know how this will actually turn out or what will happen, per se. I don't want someone to walk in on us and have their reality altered before they are ready. You know it might cause their consciousness to break because they can't handle what they see.

—I'm sorry, but if you feel that is a possible outcome for an onlooker, what is the risk for this participant?

—My Light, that is a decision you have to make for yourself. You have to determine if the risk is worth the possible reward. You have chosen wisely, My Light! Trust has always been the cornerstone of our foundation. Now take my hands, and scoot closer so our legs are in between one another. I know this is a very intimate position so I hope it is not making you uncomfortable, as this is not my intention. This technique is one you taught me, but usually, we are standing with our bodies pressed against one another.

—Like I saw in that dream when the dome appeared around us?

—Exactly, just like that! I used to think we had to be that close for it to work, but in time I've realized you did it to calm my anxiousness and fear. Placing my body on yours, feeling your heartbeat, always calmed me instantly. I believe we can sit apart to complete this technique. But I'd like to be close so I can calm you, if needed. I'd normally wait for you to awaken to the remembrance of who I am and our connection, if you awakened at all, before attempting this. But we don't have the luxury of time, like we usually have when waking the other up. Everything hangs in the balance of us finishing our mission so we must proceed onward. Close your eyes, My Light.

—Before I close my eyes, one last thing.

—Yes?

—Why do you keep calling me your light?

—No more questions, My Light. All will be clear very soon. Now, please close your eyes. Put your hands on top of mine. Silence your mind and listen only to the sound of my voice. Trust me completely! Feel my energy, and allow the energy you feel between us to consume you, creating a link from your heart to mine. Relax your mind and body and focus only on my words.

I don't remember everything before we ended up stranded on this planet! And, I know this will sound like pages out of a fiction novel. But whatever you do, please do not allow your brain to hold a seat at this meeting. I need you to stay calm and allow yourself to believe. As I talk, feel the connection between us, the depth of our unbreakable bond. Allow what I am saying to resonate in the core of your heart, to the depths of your soul. As my energy and words unlock truths hidden deep within your soul, you will remember the true depths of our trust. In time, you will start to remember and feel in every cell of your body the ancient love that is ours and ours alone. You will feel energy pulsating from your heart chakra to your crown chakra like a fresh summer breeze, raising your vibrations to a new frequency. After you have completely merged your energy with mine, in your first eye you will see our story, and in your heart, you will remember our light! I will tell you the highlights of all that I remember. The rest of our history is locked away in you, and you were helping to unlock it in me before we came here.

—I don't understand. If I knew our history, why didn't I tell you?

—You wanted me to remember on my own. You would always say it is one thing for me to describe to you the glorious wonder of sliding down rainbows, diving deep into the ocean's splendor, but it is an entirely different experience to actually partake in this event on your own. This way, you are able to not only see the memory but feel, and have a knowingness of what this experience creates in your soul to the core of your being. My Light, I would normally allow you the same grace, but we just don't have the time!

—Yes, I remember you saying we don't have time. So, let's begin then.

—Close your eyes and just breathe. I will focus my energy on you, let me know when you feel me.

—I can feel you. I can feel your energy in my heart space. I can feel strength in your soul and I can feel that same strength in me. As we sit here with our energies connected, I can literally feel our connection pulsating through my body. I trust you completely, our bond is truly unbreakable. I feel it in every fiber of my being. In my soul, I know I'd lay my life down for yours without a thought. Please continue. I promise you I will be okay.

—There was an invasion on our planet. Some of our families were lost. You found me and we fought our way off-planet. We ended up on Planet Kaytoin. We wanted to stay and help fight, but our parents advised us that we must go! Our safety and freedom were all that mattered as we were the key. You drug me away kicking and screaming!

When we turned the corner, two assassins were there. Seemingly waiting for us. I remember how in sync and fluid we fought, side by side. Once we made it to safety, we connected our energy, created a protection shield around us, made our way to our ship and we left. I don't know how I lost my memory, but yours was always fully intact. When we got to the planet Kaytoin… Well, I assume that is the first planet we arrived on as I honestly can't remember anything before that planet, other than snippets of our home planet. You were patiently waiting for me to remember. For me to remember our connection, who I am, and the fullness of my powers. Guiding me ever so patiently and lovingly along the way. But you refused to feed me my memories, you were adamant I had to remember on my own. You advised me that you telling me would be the exact same as me still not knowing, it was something I had to remember and feel deep in my soul in order for me to grasp its truth.

—How did we end up here?

—The assassins found us! We fought and came to this planet. The battle you keep seeing in your dreams is the battle we fought to get off of Planet Kaytoin, just to end up here. I don't know how, Khogee, but something went wrong, because this is not the planet we were aiming for. Somehow, we got stuck in the same cycle the inhabitants of this planet seem to be stuck in. We live a life as one character, die, and come back as a new character. However, the memories of the inhabitants are completely wiped, they remember nothing of their previous lifetime and are clueless that they are stuck in what seems like a never-ending loop. I know you think this is your first time on this merry-go-round but in reality, you have lived hundreds or thousands of times on this planet before the life you are currently living. It is as equally sad as it is infuriating. Almost seems as if we are someone's entertainment, you know a TV show they watch to pass the time.

—How are you able to remember?

—I don't know, Khogee. It is like our roles are reversed. You have now forgotten and I now remember. I don't remember every life we have lived here! But, it is always the same plot. I find you; you may wake up or you may not. Then boom we are killed shortly after. We come back into incarnation, reunite at some point, and start the process all over again.

—Wow, My Light, I…

—Open your eyes and see me! You called me your Light, why?

—I called you 'My Light' because you are the light that makes my light shine brighter. Yes, Kheira, I remember. You connecting your energy with mine woke up my heart and ignited my soul's memories, all the memories came flooding back. I know who I am and the strength and power we possess on our own and how together we amplify each other. We are even stronger together than we are apart. I also remember my last life here and how it ended. Agents have infiltrated this reality completely.

—What do you mean?

—Listen to this! In my last life, my mother killed me.

—Your mother?

—Yes, my mother. It was shortly after we reconnected and I started the process of reawakening. When I got home, she hugged me, she then looked into my eyes, deep into my soul. Then said 'You are starting to awaken! Do you know who you are?' I was so caught off guard I didn't even notice the knife in her hand. She slit my throat, then snapped my neck.

—Khogee, My Light, that is horrific. The pain, betrayal, and confusion you must have felt in that moment.

—You have no idea. As I grabbed my neck right before she snapped it, I saw tears in her eyes. Right before she finished me off, she whispered in my ear 'They will never let any of you fully remember or let you win this battle. Their thirst for power is unquenchable!' The words 'any of you' rang in my ears and stuck out while I transitioned. Why would she say 'any of you?'

—My Light, that is an interesting statement. She either means there are more pairs out there on the same or a similar mission as us, or possibly she was referring specifically to you and me. As we are on the same mission across timelines.

—How do you know this?

—Well, before I came here, I had a dream of seeing you at a restaurant. When I woke up the next day, I went to that restaurant. While there, I saw two of you. One being a clone and the other being a 'you' from another timeline. The 'you' from the other timeline saved my life at this restaurant, where we were attacked by level three agents. This other version of 'you' was sent to me from this other timeline by a 'me' from what I believe is a higher dimension, though I'm not one hundred percent sure about this fact. He let me know this is the only timeline where both of us are still alive. One or both of us have died on all other timelines. The me from the higher dimension said this has never happened, and if one of us or both of us die this time around the mission could be lost. But I don't understand how if we will all eventually recycle back in.

—I believe we both have pieces to the puzzle! If they planted agents in my life last time to kill me when I woke. Why couldn't they have done it again this lifetime, but on a grander scale, across all timelines? Maybe it took them this many years to figure out how. Now that they have, maybe their goal is to wipe us all out this lifetime so we can't succeed in eradicating them from this galaxy!

—That is a good theory, but it doesn't answer the question of us recycling back in. We'd just come back at some point and start our mission over again, right?

—Maybe not. Assuming that our energy signature would have been wiped off all timelines on this dimension in the same lifetime before any of us are able to recycle back in; what if this act makes it impossible for us to recycle back in.

—But energy doesn't die. So where would we be?

—Good point, maybe we would be stuck on a lower dimension. Think about it, we've recycled in what, hundreds or thousands of times for all we know. If we drop down a dimension, how long do you think it would take for us to get to the point where we could get back to this dimension? We could be stuck for a million years. By that time, they could have taken ownership of multiple solar systems, even the galaxy!

—My Light, this is a lot to process, and there are still so many missing pieces. Like what you were saying about agents being implanted in your last life if your theory is correct. Then, there are agents implanted into our lives now. The only person I can think of that would be an implant, is Mama G. She is the only family I have.

—Well, for me my family is very big so there are a lot of opportunities there. I also have lots of acquaintances and friends at the school we run here. It could be any one of them, or for all I know, all of them.

—No one is to be trusted! Lovely just told me that the other day, trust no one but you and her.

—Who is Lovely? That is the second time you've mentioned her?

—I see you have not lost your quickness! Lovely, is a guide who speaks to me and helps me navigate this false reality. I found out yesterday she is the 'me' from what I believe is a higher dimension.

—Let's go get food. I'm hungry. We can continue our convo and come up with our exit strategy.

—Yes, My Light, I am hungry as well. It has been a very long day. Is there any place in particular you want to go?

—There's a vegetarian spot down the way, I think you might enjoy!

Chapter 7:

Are We Safe Anywhere?

—I should have used the lady's room before we left.

—You have to go?

—Yes, badly!

—Well, we can go back or we can stop by my place on the way.

—Do you live alone? Is it safe to show up there with me?

—Good point. I live with my brother, well the person I assume is my brother. There is actually a spot right up here we can stop by. I know the owners and they keep the store very clean.

—Either way, I feel we will be taking a risk. However, I trust your judgment. Please, lead the way.

—Hi, Mr. and Mrs. Tillman. How are you today? My dear friend needs to use the restroom, is that okay?

—You know anything for you, sweet Khogee.

—Thank you. Kheira, the restroom is right over there. I will be here when you get done.

— <I am still using the restroom. You speaking to me in my heart space isn't helping the process. Can I have some privacy, please?>

— <My Light, I'm sure I've seen you naked a million times. Me talking to you while you are peeing isn't anything special. It's been a while since we've spoken to each other telepathically from our hearts, wasn't sure if

I still knew how to do it correctly. Glad to see I still know how.>

— <You picked a fine time to have a desire to practice. However, it is good to have that extra confirmation that you really remember, not that I doubted you or anything.>

— <Thank you, My Light. We need to toss everything we have on us including our phones.>

— <Why?>

— <You said you dreamed of seeing me at the restaurant, right?>

— <Yes.>

— <Then you went there, and we were ambushed?>

— <Correct.>

— <How? Did they implant that dream in your mind to make you go there? Have they been tracking you? They manipulated that situation based on data. How are they getting this data? How are they tracking you? How are they tracking us? We must get rid of everything on our person. If they put agents in our lives, I'm sure they also have tracking devices attached to our personal effects. They have probably been listening to our convos with others. And who knows they may have every word we have exchanged with one another today. We need to discuss all plans here in our heart space until we get rid of everything, and possibly even after.

I feel you thinking of my secret hideaway the other Khogee took you to. But, if you had your phone, and those clothes on. My Light, we can't stay there. We will have to come up with a Plan B, that includes us getting off this planet! And I know Suzette knows something. I felt it in her energy when she was standing beside you. I just didn't know what it was until you triggered me waking up! We must be swift and meticulous in executing our plan. Well, we will have to come up with the plan first!>

—Okay, I am done, Khogee. Let's continue this convo as we walk.

—Sounds good, but before we leave, go back in and take everything off and change. And, Kheira, I do mean everything. I got these from next door for you, along with the other essentials we need. I believe all of these items should fit just fine.

—New shoes too?

—Yes, EVERYTHING must go!

—Khogee, you remember how we got off the last planet?

—Yes, My Light, I do now. And I know where you are headed, but my concern is the same thing that happened last time will happen again. I still do not understand what went wrong. And, we can't end up on another planet, we need to go home. You spoke of a 'mission' before. What is the mission, and I am wondering if it involves this planet? I have so many questions, Kheira. But my main concern is us getting up and out of here. I feel in my gut we aren't safe here.

—Are we safe anywhere? How did they find us on Planet Kaytoin? As far as we knew, we were the only beings with a head, two arms, and two legs on Planet Kaytoin. I understand we need to leave, but it seems like we can't really run from whatever or whoever is chasing us. No matter where we go, we are found! We have to find a safe place and figure out what it is we are not seeing.

—My Light, let me think. We got rid of everything we had on us previously, except our money. We have backpacks, changes of clothes, key essentials to last us a few days, and our IDs. Okay, so let's buy a small tent and hide among the nomad community down by the bridge! I don't think anyone will look for us there. I doubt any agents are implanted in that community. But to the point made earlier, we do not understand how we are being tracked so we cannot stay there long.

—This is a good plan. Let's get the tent and the food you promised me a while ago, that I have yet to receive. Then we can head that way. In the meantime, do you think we also need to get rid of our IDs?

—I was thinking about that, My Light, but what position will that put us in if we are carded or need to buy anything that requires an ID? Honestly, I'm not sure what to do regarding the IDs.

—My Light, I feel the doubt forming in you. No matter where your choices lead us, I am by your side. I trust you completely! Don't let doubt consume you, trust yourself!

—Are you cozy in the tent, My Light?

—As cozy as can be, the food is great, and it is actually very warm in here with the sleeping bags we grabbed. Honestly, we are back together. That is all that matters to me. Have you thought any more about our next move?

—Yes, I have. I know this may sound crazy, but I think we need to go backward in order to keep going forward.

—I'm sorry, but I don't follow you.

—Well, I believe we need to project ourselves backward a few days, maybe one or two days before our planet was invaded. I don't remember every detail anymore, and I feel the key to us understanding what happened is there. Maybe we can prevent the invasion or at least stay and help our people win. Are you down, My Light?

—Know that I trust you with my life! And, would follow you anywhere, even to death! Though I feel like this plan has lots of holes in it. The idea of projecting our consciousness back in time sounds awesome. We are just missing one key ingredient to the plan.

—What do you mean?

—Khogee, we don't know how to project our consciousness back into ourselves. When I was talking to you from the other timeline you mentioned that since we left home, we have forgotten how to walk through time from one system of codes to another. This plan you are speaking of sounds like we will be attempting to travel through time. Yet I'm not sure how we will accomplish this if we have forgotten how.

—Well, actually your statement is not one hundred percent true. When you helped me to awaken back at the school, there is a memory that came back online within my consciousness. Do you remember on Planet Kaytoin, you had a vision about the rainbow water cottage in the middle of the ocean?

—Yes, I do.

—Do you remember seeing a deeply melanated being?

—Yes.

—Well, he is our master teacher! He was teaching us how to create portals. Just like the one you mentioned you saw in the cave on our walk here. The portal that future you used to walk into the cave.

—Wait, are you now proposing we create a portal and walk into a moment where there is a version of you and I in existence already? That is totally different from us projecting our consciousness backward into that moment.

—I know this may sound a little questionable and don't ask me how or why I know this, but in the memory, the one I just spoke of, I remember the instructions on what we need to do. There is a chant we can say once we open the portal. I believe the chant will automatically project our consciousness into the version of us there. Similar to what occurred for you in the dream. Your consciousness projected to a moment outside of time you were existing in at that moment.

—Okay, let's say we actually pull this off. What happens to our bodies here? Are they just going to lay in this tent unprotected for an unknown amount of time?

—Yes, My Light, there are chants we can say for all kinds of needs. We can say a chant of protection around the tent as well as one to make the tent and us invisible.

—How do you know these chants? And how come you've never used them before?

—Honestly, My Light, I didn't remember them till you brought me back online. Our teacher taught us these, and we must have somehow buried them deep within us. Let us eat, rest, and move forward with the plan in the morning. If it does not work, we will come up with plans B and C. Does that sound good?

—Yes, food and rest are this woman's dream right now.

Chapter 8:

Sama

—My Light, it is good to see you looking so refreshed this morning. Are you ready to move forward with our plan?

—I was ready last night, but after getting some rest, now I'm not sure. Khogee, why are you laughing?

—I wasn't expecting that response. My Light, do you trust me?

—From now into eternity!

—I honestly don't know if this will work. But remember, My Light, you did say you are willing to follow me anywhere, even to death.

—Thanks, Khogee. That pep talk really makes me feel even more confident in the plan now.

—My Light, let's go over the plan one more time. Make sure we both fully understand what actions and steps we must take to pull this off. Remember, I will stand here and focus my mind and heart on the exact moment we are returning to.

—My Light, when is this moment again?

—A week before the war broke out on our home planet. Kheira, do you want to hear the plan or not?

—Yes, of course. I apologize for my interruption.

—As I was saying, then we will start the hand mudras I showed you last night to open the portal. From there we will say the chant: 'Aye I Moaya Layme!' This should project us into the 'us' there.

—Sounds good. Now can you tell me what our mission is again?

—My Light, are you stalling with all these clarifying questions?

—Umm, of course, I am, but I also want to ensure we both thoroughly understand the plan. I don't want my consciousness to end up inside of a rock or a leaf blowing in the wind.

—You know the mission. It is to stop the invasion and figure out what pieces of the puzzle we currently do not know. So, are you ready now?

—Yes, My Light. I am.

—Let's start by making the hand mudra with our left hand to bend the construct of this program. Bend your pinkie and ring finger down. Hold your index finger and middle finger straight up and then bend your thumb in. Great job! Now with your right hand, we will bring our thumb, pinkie, and ring together weaving our hands in circles. We will use our middle and index fingers to control the motion of the path!

—Wow! This is actually working. Look there! I see us in the sky having a sparring session. Watch! This is when I'm about to kick your butt!

—My Light, focus! We can relive that moment in a few! Start the chant!

—I cannot believe it worked. Not saying I was doubting you or anything. This is so amazing. I feel like my old self again! Look at us, we are here in our bodies flying in the clouds! And I am still about to kick your butt.

—Ha! Funny, Kheira, you couldn't kick my butt if you tried. The last five hundred centuries well attest to this.

—Seriously though, I didn't know what to expect. I wasn't sure if my consciousness was going to end up in your body, in a tree, or what. But it actually worked.

—So, what I am hearing from you right now, is that you didn't believe in me?

—My Light, I always believe in you. My trust in you is deeper than the ocean! It was just your technique I was doubting.

—My technique, aye? Try this technique out and let me know how you like it.

—Khogee, did you just shoot a fireball at me? How is that possible?

—You say you feel like your old self again yet you can't remember your full power. Kheira, anything you can imagine or conceive you can do! All you have to do is believe! Your power—our power—is beyond your wildest imagination. And when we are in full power, fighting side by side, we are a sight to behold. Like watching water dance at the top of an ocean wave, moving in and out of form, transforming into a raging dragon ready to attack any foe who stands in its way!

—I don't understand how you are fully connected to who you are, but I'm not.

—Well, My Light, you are floating in the air right now. You have to be connected to the fullness of who you are in some kind of way. I think the issue is that you are blocked internally. I'm not sure what is causing the block, but I have an idea how we may be able to remove it once and for all. My Light, take my hand! Close your eyes and breathe deeply for four seconds, and exhale for another four seconds. Keep breathing deeply until you connect to the essence of who you are. Once you have made that connection, and are fully present in this moment and clear of mind. Then open your eyes. Now, look me in my eyes, deep into my soul, until you feel our love consuming you from the inside out. Good, Kheira, I feel you in my heart space. Listen to me carefully in your heart space. Don't let fear or doubt consume you! Trust yourself and trust me, I will never knowingly or purposefully cause you harm. On this journey we are about to take, I need you to be present and clear of mind. Do you understand, My Light?

—Yes, My Light, I do.

—Great, we are going to start off by flying up high then we are going to dive deep, into the depths of the ocean! I believe this will be just the trick to remove that block keeping you from connecting to the fullness of who you are. You ready?

—Yes!

—I feel your excitement. Let's go, I'll race you to the top of that cloud shaped like twin trees. Once there, we will fly down and dive deep into the water. Stay close to me so I don't lose you. If I'm going too fast at any time, or you want to stop and look around, let me know.

—Wait. So, we can breathe underwater too?

—My Light, beyond your wildest dreams, don't forget that! You ready? On three, we move.

—Mmmmm, the wind against my face as we raced felt so refreshing!

—My Light, I'm glad you are enjoying yourself, and your speed is picking up tremendously! You stayed right beside me the entire time, no lag at all.

—Thank you! My Light! Wow, Khogee, this cloud is amazing! Two trees intertwined side by side. It is perfect like someone hand sculpted this image!

—Interesting choice of words.

—What do you mean?

—Someone did sculpt this, but they didn't use their hands. They used their light.

—Really, who?

—Us, My Light! We did this!

—I don't understand why or should I say how?

—When we were nine— Wait, before I start, do you remember how I told you about how we perished in the volcano!

—Yes, My Light, I do.

—Well, when we came back, around the age of nine or so, we started to remember or—should I say awaken—to the connection and depth of our bond. The pureness and ancientness of our love. One day while playing down by the ocean. We decided to create a solar system in the sand. During the excavation and creation process our hands touched, and we immediately looked into each other's eyes. While looking into each other's eyes… well, the best way I can explain is an immense amount of energy started to gather in our heart chakras. As we continued to gaze into each other's souls, this intense energy in our heart chakras started to build upon itself and eventually moved upward to our crown chakra. As I leaned in and kissed you, a huge explosion erupted out of our crown chakras. Shooting light straight into the sky. The light coming out of me and the light coming out of you intertwined with each other and hit this cloud creating the sculpture before your eyes. Don't ask me how this is possible, none of the elders knew either. They've never seen anything like it before or sense. They were just glad the light hit this cloud and it transformed the energy as they aren't sure what would have or could have happened if the cloud didn't absorb the light.

—Wow, Khogee! I am speechless.

—You speechless, come here and let me feel your forehead. I need to make sure you aren't coming down with something.

—Really! Stop it, Khogee.

—Okay, My Light, seriously. It is time now. Embrace your power and stay present. If any doubt or fear arises breathe through it, and on the exhale release the fear! You ready?

—Yes! Let's dive! <Wow, this feels amazing! The water surrounding my skin feels like a familiar old friend. I can feel what the eyes can't see, pure indescribable magic! I hear a soft melody playing in the water with every movement, such a lovely tune. I can see with my first eye, memories embedded in every note. Memories from many ages ago that we no

longer have recollection of. Khogee, My Light, do you feel, do you hear, can you see everything I'm experiencing? The water is guiding me as though it remembers me!>

— <I'm right here with you. Allow the water to guide you, allow her to remove the block keeping your memories at bay. She will lead the way, all you have to do is follow her and trust her, and I will trust and follow you, My Light!>

<Kheira, look where your old friend has brought you.>

— <Where? This place looks so familiar to me, but I'm not sure where we are or what this place is.>

— <Come, let's go inside. Maybe walking around and seeing familiar faces you know and places you have been will help.>

—Khogee, I now remember! This is one of our training facilities for level one warriors.

—You are coming back to yourself I see.

—I wonder, why is it so empty in here? Seems like there would be more individuals down here. Probably still in class based on the time of day.

—You up to finishing the sparring match we were just engaged in? You know, finish that butt whooping you said you were going to put on me!

—You must be eager to get embarrassed, you know I am always up for a session with you. Let's get changed, and guess what?

—Yes, My Light! I remember where my locker is. Meet you back here in ten minutes!

—Wow, you are really dressed for a sparring session. I see you weren't lying. You actually did remember where your locker is.

—You got jokes I see.

—Come now, stop with the stalling, and let's begin. Do you remember how we started our sessions?

—Of course, I do.

—Show me then.

—You are trying to trip me up, My Light, because I can't show you. The first move is always on you.

—Is it really? Tell me what to do then.

—First, you get on your knees and bow down to the floor before me. Then I get on my knees and bow down to the floor before you. Then we embrace and kiss. Always, in this order! And then as usual I thrash you.

—Wow! I am impressed, My Light. You seem to be your old self again; other than this delusion you have about being able to beat me. However, I know a quick sparring session will reveal if you are truly back or if this is a façade.

—Well, stop talking then and get to bowing, so I can show you, My Light.

—Kheira and Khogee, I thought that was you two!

—Hey Mishona, how have you been?

—I have been great. I was wondering why the two of you were not in our element's session today. You really missed a special lesson. Today Mother Scion herself was present, she has mastered the use of elements in warfare. Today was the first day of her session but she will be here for a month working with us. In today's lesson, we learned how to take water and manipulate it into different weapons.

—Mishona, why are you bothering these two with the details of our weapons class? Don't you know they are the top two ranked warriors on our level? They have taken, excelled in, and mastered every class offered.

They can wield and manipulate every element you can think of, plus some. Can't you tell by their different colored regalia? They adorn the color purple to signify they are considered master warriors. Which is the top-class level within the warrior one class.

—Thank you, Shinaya, for the quick history lesson that I did not ask for. I am well aware of who they are and what their different colored regalia means, as you say! But as our Master Teacher has informed us on many occasions, you should never stop adding knowledge to your database.

—What are you trying to say, Mishona?

—Shinaya, I said it clearly, but just so you do not miss the message, they may have benefited from the lesson as she may have had different perspectives than their previous teacher.

—Mishona and Shinaya, from the sounds of things the two of you need to take this sparring session instead of myself and Kheira. Please, let us step off the mat so the two of you can take over.

—Mishona, would you like to spar?

—Yes, Shinaya! I am always ready. Let's begin!

—Kheira and Khogee, I thought that was you. Sama has requested your presence in his chamber. Mishona and Shinaya, please move on to your next lesson and I will be there momentarily to assist you with stretches. We will not have any sparring matches today.

—Yes, Yogesh, right away!

—Kheira and Khogee, I suggest you make haste.

—Khogee, master warriors? That sure sounds impressive.

—My Light, focus.

—I always appreciate how you keep me balanced, My Light. Do you have any thoughts on why Sama has requested our presence?

—I have no idea. I am just as clueless as you.

—You don't think he knows, do you?

—Considering who we are speaking of nothing is out of the question, but I am not sure how he would know since we just got here, and have not been in his presence yet.

—Come in, Kheira and Khogee. It is good to see the two of you. Please shut the door and take a seat. And to answer the question you were discussing as you approached, yes, I do know! I know that you are not the Kheira and Khogee from this moment in time. Which is why I have requested your presence. You should not be here and must leave at once.

—Sama, can you please help us to understand why?

—Khogee, if you search the crevices of your heart, you will find the answer you seek.

—With the utmost respect, Sama, can you please help us unravel the riddle? If time is not on our side, I would prefer not to waste it figuring out what you already know.

—The reasoning you have for traveling backward is very sound but you missed one key piece of information in your thought process. Everything has played out the way it has for a reason. How do you know that you have not in a more forward moment come back and changed the flow of events? If that is the case, how do you know your actions currently are not being influenced outside of yourself in an effort to undo what has and will be done? Furthermore, how do you know that I have not already accounted for the manipulation in time you are now facing and haven't already gone forward to future moments to correct the manipulation in an effort to ensure the two of you do not fail at your mission?

—Sama, who are you? How could you have known we are not the Kheira and Khogee from this moment in time if you haven't even seen us until this moment? And how do we protect ourselves from being influenced unknowingly by what is outside of us?

—Kheira, you and Khogee never cease to amaze me with your capacity to see what most miss. Your keen sense of observation will be one of the key catalysts in helping you both with the successful completion of your mission. Never underestimate the power of silent observation from a place of purity and peace. To answer your first question, you have seen me in my true form in the colorful water cottage, Kheira. Stay on course, when you fully remember who you are you will know who I am and have always been. To answer your last question second. I will be sure to assist you both with this before you leave. Now to answer your second question last, I felt the wave you all caused in the energy field when you entered into this moment in time. A very subtle ripple effect, but an effect nonetheless.

—Sama, thank you for patiently answering my and Kheira's questions. If you would please grant us the grace of more of your patience. After pondering your previous comments about why we cannot be here. I still don't quite understand why us being here is a bad thing. Even if in a more forward moment we came back into this moment and changed things, how could us coming back before that moment impact anything? The us in that forward moment would remember we came back in this moment and accounted for any corrections that needed to be made.

—Khogee, forever the introspective pupil. I told you your keen gift of observation will take you far, you and Kheira always see what others miss. Now that I know you both are fully present in this moment, we may begin our true conversation. The two of you cannot change the events that have occurred here in these moments, as doing so will cause you to fail your mission when you go back to the moment you left, in order to be in this moment. Though painful, the events that preceded you all being stuck on Saynohs were needed to get both of you where you are now, on track to successfully complete your mission. Never lose faith in yourselves or each other. Hold strong to the unconditional trust you have in each other, never allow it to waiver. It is your foundation. Never allow anyone to plant seeds of doubt that could cause it to break! I must send the two of you back now! Before you go, I will place more light in both of you. Aimed to increase your power and strengthen your connection to each other! Remember my words, no matter what happens as you move forward on your journey, know in the depths of your soul that the foundation between the two of you can never be broken by anyone. Unless you allow someone to trick the two of you into breaking it yourselves! Loyalty is always required, remember this, my children! The next time you see me, do not see me! In any situation where you need my guidance, speak to me from your heart space. Know that I am always just a thought away.

Chapter 9:

Welcome Home

— <Khogee, My Light, can you hear me?>

— <Yes, My Light, I can.>

— <Where are you, where are we?>

— <I'm not sure, Kheira. I know we are not back in the tent where we originally left our bodies, yet we are back in our bodies. This container I'm in has no light source whatsoever. It is completely black in here! But, My Light, I feel you and that gives me comfort.>

— <Yes, I feel you too, and it does bring calmness to this uncertain situation. I wonder what happened? I thought when we jumped back, we'd be in our tent brainstorming the next phase of our plan?>

— <This is just an assumption, but based on our current circumstances, I believe our bodies were discovered and confiscated.>

— <Really, you pick now to be smart-lipped.>

— <Sorry, what else can we do in this moment but make light of this uncertain situation? However, we do need to figure out who confiscated us, and where exactly we are going. It seems so odd as to how we were discovered when we put protection spells and made our tent and bodies invisible.>

— <The only thing I can think of is that the ones who confiscated them know the same magic you used, and how to reverse it. Wait, I can feel us slowing down. I believe we will find out sooner than later where exactly we are. I hear footsteps approaching toward us.>

— <Kheira, remember your training. Stay docile, allow your enemy to underestimate you! When the time is right, do what you do best!>

—Kheira and Khogee, welcome home! We have truly missed both of you and are glad to have you back. Please, come with us, let's get you both cleaned and changed so we can properly welcome you home.

—Excuse me, who are you and where are we as this is most assuredly not our home.

—Oh, my dear Khogee, I assure you this is the home of your original inception. You just have been under so long you have forgotten.

—Under?

—Yes, undercover. Embedded as our top-level spies. Don't worry we will refresh your memories in our memory restoration chamber. Simple name, I know, but do not let the simplicity of the name fool you into underestimating the power within. How rude of me, I have not introduced myself as of yet. I am Alcarekh, the chief host. I am here to assist you with your every whim. If you continue to follow me, we will make our way over to the wash area where you will be properly cleaned, and have your body adorned to a standard that will meet our level of sophistication. From there you will end up at the memory restoration chamber. You both can go in together or you can go in separately. Either way, the result of the experience will be the same, you will be cleaned, with acceptably adorned bodies. Now please step forward.

— <Kheira, give me your hand. Let's go through together, this way we will be together and can protect one another.>

— <You know this all feels so familiar to me but something seems off all at the same time.>

— <I know, My Light. I agree with you wholeheartedly. He tells us we have returned to our home, yet our arrival required us to be placed in sealed containers with absolutely no light source. I'd say there is definitely something off. Until we know more and can fully assess this situation, let's stay together and entertain the pompousness of Alcarekh. Quickly we will figure out our best routes of escape. Do you understand

our current plan? If so, let me know when you are ready to move forward.>

— <Yes, My Light, I'm ready to move forward through this so-called wash area.>

—Great. I am glad to see the two crowns in waiting are being so cooperative. Now, let's see. Do you want to go through one at a time or together?

—We will go through together.

—Excellent, Khogee. Now if we can have the two of you step onto the hovering platform. Now place both of your feet shoulder-width apart. This platform will move you through the wash area on its own. At the end, you will see mechanic arms appear that will adorn you in appropriate attire. All you need to do is stand still and allow yourselves to enjoy the magic known only to and specialized in by our higher species, the Kashnoths. Before you go, I would like to also point out the railing in front of you. I suggest you hold on to it, just in case the ride starts to get bumpier than anticipated. We will be awaiting your arrival on the other side of the veil.

—Interesting, I thought the platform would have taken us forward not upward.

— <Kheira, I know we seem to be alone, but I am not sure we are. Please, continue to speak to me here, in our heart space only. Even when it seems we are by ourselves. I believe this precaution is needed until we know for sure that we can trust for our words to be heard.>

— <Yes, of course, My Light, your intuition is always sound. Look Khogee, do you see this? Small orbs of light are falling upon our bodies as we move through this blacked out tunnel. It feels tantalizing and refreshing all at the same time. I wonder where they are coming from as I do not see their source of origination. They seem to just materialize from thin air. Look there are more and they all have the same mission, to find a permanent home on our bodies.>

— <What color are the orbs you see?>

— <I see green, blue, and purple orbs of light.>

— <I want to see if we are experiencing the same thing, and I see that we are not. The orbs that I see are yellow, orange, and red. I'm curious if this is some kind of simulation being projected into our mind or if this is real.>

— <He did say to enjoy the magic of Kashnoths, Khogee. Maybe this is a part of the magic. We are perceiving and receiving experiences unique to us as individuals. Though as I said earlier your intuition is always sound. Let's test your simulation theory, tell me what you are seeing now.>

— <I see us as children, holding hands, running and playing in a field of yellow sunflowers. Now tell me what you see.>

— <I see pure blackness, punctuated by brightly illuminated stars of orange, purple, yellow, red, green, and blue light! I also see portals opening from three different directions. I believe a choice needs to be made and my intuition is telling me it's the one on the left. My heart does not disagree.>

— <Kheira, wait! Don't move, before we go any further. Let's go over Alcarekh's words. I believe he said 'We will make our way over to the wash area... from there you will end up at the memory restoration chamber.'>

— <Yes, you are correct, those were his words. Is the implication that we are in the memory restoration chamber now?>

— <That's a great question. I assumed he meant we would come to the wash area, completely finish there, and then we would be escorted to the memory restoration chamber. However, this assumption could have been wrong. What if the wash area is the gate we must walk through, and the portals you are now seeing are how we access what they call the memory restoration chamber? Think about it, he called us the 'crowns'

and said we are top level spies from this planet, maybe this is a test to see if we remember our path here on this planet.>

— <Quick thinking, then what exactly was the wash area?>

— <I believe it washed the illusion we were perceiving from our minds. Look at your body and look at mine, we are now the same color as the orbs you saw with our attire also matching the color of the orbs.>

— <Interesting, though I didn't see any mechanical hands pop out. Unless the orbs are what he was referring to as mechanical hands. I see I am different shades of green, blue, and purple fading in and out of each other all over my body. I was so mesmerized by what was taking place before my eyes. I have not laid my eyes on you in a while to notice the same has happened to your skin but in the tones of yellow, orange, and red. And you are right, our attire does match the same color scheme as our skin. What a magnificent sight to behold but also a strange turn of events.>

— <It's only strange because of what we have been accustomed to seeing on the hell planet we've been stuck on for so long, My Light!>

— <You are right, Khogee. As we take in more of where we are from here on our home planet, I'm sure the normal feeling will come back to us.>

— <Well, My Light, I don't know about the 'where we are from' thing just yet. You remember on Kaytoin before we were trapped on Saynohs you had a dream of home where you ended up in a cottage in the middle of the ocean made of colored water?>

— <Yes, I remember.>

— <Well, do you also remember the way our true forms looked when you saw us at the cottage in the middle of the ocean, as deeply melanated as the cosmos? Not the colors we currently see. Something is still not all the way right, maybe all of this is a simulation. I am not one hundred percent sure either way, but regardless we must continue to move forward. For now, let's go with the flow and see what unfolds before us. Until then, you know the code, we trust no one but each other. Now

back to these portals, Kheira, I believe your intuition and heart were providing you with direction on which portal we should choose.>

— <Yes, My Light, my soul seems to remember the way, but I'm doubting my intuition. I'm being guided to the left portal. However, what happens if I'm wrong? And if I am, what awaits us on the other side?>

— <I trust you and your intuition completely, My Light. I need you to trust your own intuition the same way you trust mine. Take my hand and follow me, let's move with urgency. I don't want to stay in this space any longer than we have to. I'm not sure what will happen if we take too long to make a choice. I know we are not sure of what awaits on the other side of either of these portals. However, I believe waiting here will deal us a potentially worse fate. It feels as though we might get stuck in an endless loop if we do not hastily make a decision. Time is of the essence, My Light.>

— <Now that we are inside of the left portal, I'll tell you what I see, and then ask that you do the same. Let us make sure we are not having the same experience we just had in the wash area. I am currently seeing the portal moving around us in a clockwise motion. The portal seems to be made of swirling goldish-white light. The more we move the swirls of goldish-white light are starting to form pictures.>

— <Yes, I am seeing the exact same thing. Please continue your description. If anything you say seems to be different from what I am seeing, I will let you know.>

— <Okay, I am now seeing images of what seems to be us growing up here on this planet from childhood into adulthood. Wait, I see the swirls of goldish-white light are now starting to come toward us. It seems to be electrified with gold sparks flying everywhere.>

—Kheira and Khogee, my name is Aynobe, and I will be your conductor as you move through the memory restoration chamber. I will be the one to provide you both with a full restoration of your memories. Please do not be afraid, I am the swirling goldish-white light you see all around you. My lightning rods you see coming toward you are going to insert themselves at key points in your body. You may know these points as energy centers, though my lightning rods are electrified you will feel no pain. Once they have entered your memory centers, you will blackout completely. When you come to, you will have regained full memory of who you are and the royal seats you hold on Kashnoths. Do either of you have any questions before we begin?

—Yes, I do have one question. What do you mean by royal seats?

—Kheira, I do understand the two of you have been gone for quite a while and have lost all of your memories. Once you have completed the full restoration process you will know exactly what I mean by royal seats! However, I will entertain this one question with patience before we begin the full memory restoration. You and Khogee are the offspring of the two chief families that rule the Planet Kashnoths. Therefore, you are both crowns. Granting each of you a royal seat amongst the Kashnoths Imperial Royal Council without question. Now if there are no questions about the process, I beg of you to stay calm and grounded as this process starts. Know that you will not feel any pain and are safe. Shall we begin?

—Do we have any choice in this matter?

—Of course! You and Khogee always have a choice, free will if I may. It is the consequences of the choice you must ponder upon, rather than focusing on the choice itself.

—Are you at liberty to tell us what those consequences may be?

—One will lead to freedom on Kashnoths and the other to your demise, choose wisely.

—Well, based on your feedback it seems moving forward will be the best course of action. I see this choice as the most adequate decision considering the consequences involved.

—Kheira, I assume you speak on both you and Khogee's behalf, as I have not heard him mutter a word as of yet.

—Yes, she does, Aynobe. Always.

—Excellent choice! Now, before we get started, I beg of you both to listen to my instructions very carefully and follow them to the letter.

First, I need you to breathe in deeply for ten counts. Once you reach the tenth count, hold your breath. Then place your tongue on the roof of your mouth. Close your eyes, and allow your mind to relax completely, taking your conscious awareness deep into your body. You two are doing great, now that I feel in your energy you are at the place of complete soul awareness, I will begin entering your energy centers. May you both find peace in the freedom of knowing who you truly are.

Chapter 10:

Restoration Chamber

—My Light, are you finally coming back from the ethers?

—Khogee, how long have I been out?

—We were both out for quite a while. I traveled for about two days and you have been traveling for about three days. Before you get up look me in my eyes and tell me what you know, My Light. This way we can compare notes.

—Yes, of course. As I look deep into your eyes, I know you!

— <I know I was just speaking to you audibly in the previous moment, but please speak to me here, in our heart space, as you tell me about your journeys. I am still not sure who we can trust. I do apologize for interrupting you, My Light, please continue.>

— <Yes, I understand your trepidation, but we are amongst our rightful family now, and can trust them. This will be the last thing I say to you here in our sacred heart space.> My Light. Sorry for the pause; I guess traveling for three days took a little more out of me than I realized. However, after this journey and experiencing so many genuine authentic moments of pure unconditional openness and thoughtfulness, I now understand. I now understand why I know, see, and completely feel the depths of who you are within the itching of my soul. I will never trust anyone more than I trust you and will follow you anywhere. Our connection is deeper than I could have ever imagined. Everything we have and are to one another is built upon trust. In all things, we trust each other completely. In this moment, every moment behind us and in front of us, our trust in one another always reassures us. We always have the best interest of the other in mind, when making any decisions. We always submit to each other, there is never a power struggle between us, My Light! Our intuition has never led either of us astray and the moments in front of us will be no different. Do you understand, Khogee?

—Yes, of course, I do. My Light. Please continue; you have my full attention.

—During my travels, I was able to restore all that had been lost of my memory. And, you have always been here with me, My Light! I saw that we are of a royal lineage. We are ancient and have been lovers for as far back as I was allowed to travel. Due to the longevity of our bond and the depth of trust we have in one another, we were tasked with fulfilling a mission of infiltrating the Isonateon planet. Our parents knew this mission would be a long one and there would be only one way two individuals could partake in this mission together and make it back as one. They had to have ultimate and complete loyalty to one another. You see, the Isonateon civilization stole the Saynohs' planet from Kashnoths. When we fled from Isonateon and crash-landed on Kaytoin, it was our people, the Kashnoths who attacked the Isonateons. They were not trying to harm us as we had been told by our fake parents on Isonateon. They were indeed coming to rescue us as well as defeat those who cheated them in battle.

You see, time's past, the Kashnoths discovered the planet Isonateon. The planet was uninhabited by a superior intelligent life form. The Kashnoths Imperial Royal Council, seeing this as an opportunity for them to grow their dynasty, made the decision to take this planet as their own. Two families of the council's four chief families decided to develop and start their new home. These two families were the House of Khininten and the House of Kheynoos. This left two chief families here to rule over the planet Kashnoths, the heads of these two families are our parents. You come from the House of Khostempain I come from the house of Khininten. Over time the four chief families decided to continue in their exploration, with the goal of finding other planets to take under their wing. They came across the planet Saynohs and decided that it would be another great opportunity for them to grow their dynasty. There was only one problem—this planet already had inhabitants and owners. The owners of the Saynohs planet were the Eclanites, and they were not willing to part with their property. No amount of persuading or offerings enticed them into changing their mind. The Kashnoths waged a great battle against the Eclanites for they were determined to take ownership of this planet, as they wanted to take over the experiment currently taking place there. You and I both were able to get a taste of this experiment. With what seemed like never-ending cycles of being born, taken out of the game, and placed back in as a new character with no memory of the last character you played. Though I understand the details of the experiment I am still not clear as to its purpose.

There was a difference in opinion on what to do with the Saynohs planet. The two chief clans on Isonateon wanted to continue down the same path the Eclanites were on when they took over the ownership of Saynohs. By continuing to study the inhabitants of Saynohs in order to come up with a way to help free them from the endless cycle they seemed to be stuck in. The Isonateon chief scientist was all on board and ready to assist in any way possible with a viable plan to free the Saynohtians. However, the two chief clans of Kashnoths did not want this outcome and wanted things to continue as they were. Despite their differences, the four chief families of Kashnoths fought side by side. The Kashnoths clans won the battle against the Eclanites and took ownership of Saynohs. They had plans to continue the ongoing experiment as well as develop further plans on how they could increase in benefit from this planet. However, there was a betrayal of the worst kind that took place. The two chief Kashnoths clans, who are now officially known as the Isonateons, had secretly developed a different kind of magic they'd been perfecting in secret. The Isonateon magic was able to defeat that of the Kashnoths. As a result, the Isonateons were able to take ownership of Saynohs. To ensure that they were not harmed. And that no future battles would be waged against them for ownership of Saynohs, the Isonateons placed a curse on the Kashnoths' two chief families. This curse would cause immediate death to the entire lineage of Kashnoths' chief family if anyone from Kashnoths stepped foot on Isonateon.

This is where we come in. Our chief scientist was able to develop a way to project our consciousness into the two Isonateon chief clan's toddler children. Bypassing their death curse 'if any Kashnoths stepped foot on Isonateon.' As technically we would be in the body of Isonateons. The goal was for us to retain our full faculties, grow up and gain their trust, learn the science behind the curse they placed on our lineage, and reverse it before they even realized what happened. However, something went wrong on transport. We ended up in the fetuses being birthed by the

Isonateon chief clans' mothers instead of their toddlers. As a result, all memory of who we are and where we truly come from was lost. Except the one memory ingrained in our subconscious; to learn their magic and reverse the 'death curse.' We were able to succeed in our mission and this is when the battle was waged by Saynohs to take over Isonateon and bring us home. However, we fled which caused suspicion and concern in the minds of our parents. As they did not understand the intention behind nor the rationale of our actions. Can you confirm if what I am telling you so far lines up with the memory that was restored in you?

—Yes, Kheira, this is exactly how I remember things as well.

—Great, My Light, I am glad we are both finally on the same page!

—Yes, I must agree it truly feels amazing for us both to finally be at the same place in what we know and recall without any blind spots or black holes. I would love to pick your brain more about why you think the Eclanites started the experiment currently underway on planet Saynohs.

—I would love to engage in a deep retrospective conversation with you, but I am currently exhausted. And, I know I have been under for three days traveling, but I need more rest. Can you please come back when it is dark outside? We can take one of our late night walks and at that time tackle the deep thoughts and ponderings you have regarding the Eclanites.

—If that is what you wish. I will see you later tonight when it is dark.

—Thank you for understanding, My Light. I will see you shortly. Oh, can you please set the lights to lilac as you leave? The purple tones really help with calming my mind and expediting my rest state.

—Of course, anything else you need before I leave.

—No, that will be all.

Chapter 11:

Protection Sigil

— <Khogee, My Light, I hope you can truly hear me, here in your heart space. If you can please don't divert your eyes or do anything outside of the normal that would make anyone, or anything for that matter, think you are having an internal conversation with me. I am concerned that the memory restoration chamber may have given way to this gift we share, as I know it tried to eradicate our true memories. My Light, why are you not responding? Please tell me you can hear me. Khogee, are you there? Speak to me!>

— <My Light. I am here.>

— <My heart almost jumped out of my chest. What took you so long to respond?>

— <I was being escorted back to my room by two agents. I was doing two things. One, waiting to see if they gave off any kind of hint that they were aware you were communicating with me. Second, I did not want to give them any kind of hint, in my eye movement or energy field, that I was communicating with you in my heart space. After our convo in your room, I wasn't sure if they were in the dark about this gift or not. But if they are in the dark, I would like to leave them in that place.>

— <Yeah. I am not sure if that so-called memory restoration chamber allowed them to see into, and read us while they were restoring their chosen memories. Which is why when you spoke to me in our heart space while in my room, I made sure to make comments that would be flattering to the Kashnoths, if they were listening. However, no one busted in the room. So, I believe we are safe.>

— <I agree. Based on how the guards did not give off any hint they knew you were secretly communicating with me. I believe we are good. I am not going to lie though, Kheira, you had me worried for a minute.

I thought maybe whatever they were attempting to do to us in the memory restoration chamber actually took in you. However, my heart was steadfast in our trust and very observant. I knew you didn't preface the details of your journey with so many statements about our trust, submission, intuition, and lack of power struggle for no reason.>

— <My Light, I am so thankful you are always in tune with me. Ever the observant one, always catching what others miss. You have no idea how relieved I am that our connection remains intact.>

— <Thank you, My Light, it feels good to be seen. Now that we are truly on the same page, tell me what you truly know.>

— <Khogee, before we get to what I know. What are you doing?>

— <Following your lead, My Light. I am laying in my chambers with my light set to lilac, mimicking a state of rest just like you. I assume you believe there are cameras here where we take rest, in addition to not being a hundred percent sure if they discovered our sacred space where we communicate. Before your previously stated confirmation, this is the only explanation I could think of as to why you spoke to me audibly after my request for us to speak in our sacred space. And why you laid down and pretended to take rest while you contacted me privately! Considering that you did contact me you must be confident they are still unaware of this gift we share.>

— <My Light, I love you deeply! I love how you always comprehend my verbal and non-verbal clues. Now this is what I know. Listen carefully. When we last saw Sama, do you remember what he advised us?>

— <Of course, he said he would put light in us aimed at helping to increase our power and connection to one another.>

— <Yes, that is exactly what he said. When the goldish-white light, that called itself Aynobe, inserted its lighting rods in our key energy centers. The first thing I saw before I blacked out was the light placed in us by Sama. I knew it was the light Sama placed in us because it radiated more vibrant and brilliant than the light of Aynobe. The light of Sama also felt nurturing and healing, like all knowing laid within its splendor. In this light, I saw what looked like different oblong shapes making up what I

recognized from our training on Isonateon as a hidden protection sigil. I know this sigil is what protected both of us and prevented our true memory from being erased. Though what we saw is true, it is only a partial truth told from the side of the Kashnoths. I know there is so much more to the story of Kashnoths' ancient history. Without Sama's protection sigil, a lot of what we have learned and acquired since we left here would have completely been eradicated and replaced with only the memories they wish for us to retain.>

— <I agree! I notice you said 'Kashnoths' ancient history.' Do you no longer subscribe to the belief that this is our home of origin?>

— <No, My Light, I do not. What I said about us being ancient and being lovers for as far back as I was allowed to travel is true. I will never trust anyone more than I trust you, My Light.>

— <How do you know this was not an implant as well?>

— <Because I saw the same sigil flash before my eyes right before I saw this memory and after. It was divinely protected. However, Khogee, I do know something is off by the manipulation attempted while we were in the memory restoration chamber.>

— <I am glad to hear that. Again, I agree with you wholeheartedly. When I was traveling I saw the same sigil of protection you saw. The sigil appeared to me in the form of a door made of brilliant light with the sigil decorating the front of the door. I stared at the door for a moment caught up in the beauty radiating from the light. I heard a sweet melody playing in my heart and heard the light speak to me, beckoning me to come forth and enter. When I opened the door, to my amazement I saw you and I. And, you will never guess where we were.>

— <Where?>

— <We were back at the cottage in the middle of the ocean. We were bowing before our Master Teacher. And you will never guess what he said to us. Listen to his words carefully. 'Thank you for signing up for this mission. I know this mission is not an easy one but is needed to keep balance. Success of this mission will prevent the total destruction of a solar system. When your journey grows weary and the door within your

mind is left open for doubt to creep in, remember my words. No matter what happens as you move forward on your journey. Know in the depths of your soul that the foundation your bond is built upon can never be broken by anyone. Unless you allow someone else to trick you into breaking it yourselves! Loyalty is always required and feeds the fire of trust between the two of you that fans the flames of your love. It is your loyalty to one another and trust in each other that will see you through to success.' Does that sound familiar to you?>

— <Yes, those words are along the same words Sama told us the last time we were in his presence.>

— <Exactly, My Light. I have been pondering the implications behind the two events since I came back from my two days of traveling in the ethers, collecting the memories Aynobe wanted me to capture. I am thankful the sigil of protection provided by Sama gave me a back door to see one of our more ancient moments.>

— <In my brief moment of pondering your words, the only conclusion I can come to is that our Master Teacher and Sama are one and the same!>

— <This too has been my conclusion as well. This conclusion would explain a lot. He is beyond anyone we know in all of his abilities. How else can you explain him knowing the details of the conversation we had in our sacred heart space before we arrived at the door of his office back on Isonateon? We have never run across anyone with the ability to hear our secret convos. To me that shows he is more advanced than anyone we have ever met, including those on this planet called the Kashnoths.>

— <I agree wholeheartedly, My Light! I know there is still so much to dissect about the greatness of the being we call Sama, but my mind is currently distracted with how we get out of here. Have you had a chance to think of a plan of escape yet? I have several thoughts myself. One thought is we can recreate the same event we created on Saynohs, but instead of projecting our consciousness into different versions of us we just walk through. Though I'm not sure how we'd pull that off. However, at the same time, I feel deeply we are here for a reason. You know, what you saw during your two days of traveling. The mission you heard Sama speak of. What if part of our mission is on Kashnoths. Based on what

we both saw in the memory restoration chamber. They have allowed their thirst for power to consume them, ultimately feeding the darkness that exists in them while at the same time breeding more. Their goal is not to spread love and light, but only forced submission, slavery, and fear. Just look at how they are handling Saynohs since they have recently taken over ownership. Though it may be uncomfortable for the moment, I do believe we need to stay here until our souls urge us to leave. What are your thoughts, Khogee, do you agree?>

— <Yes, I agree with your sound reasoning. I too feel that there is a purpose for us here. I am just not sure what direction this purpose is currently guiding us. My suggestion is that we take a rest for the night. We can see how tomorrow unfolds and regroup again at night under our lilac light, My Light. Kheira.>

— <Yes.>

— <Stay connected to me here in our heart space as you take a rest. I need to feel you!>

— <I don't like being separated from you like this either. I will stay connected to you throughout the night so we can bring each other comfort and peace, My Light!>

Chapter 12:

Worth the Risk

— <Kheira, My Light, are you back from your nightly travels?>

— <Yes, My Light. I am wide awake, bright-eyed and bushy-tailed. How are you feeling this morning?>

— <Feeling great, waiting to see what this day has in store. Do you still have guards outside your chambers?>

— <Yes, I do. Wait a second one of the agents is announcing they are coming in.>

—Excuse me, Kheira. The heads of the house of Khininten and Khostempain are requesting the presence of you and Khogee. If you will, please take a moment to properly prepare yourself. You will find suitable attire behind the door on the far east wall and all the other needed accommodations in the wash area through the door on your left. We will give you forty-five minutes to ready yourself. Then we will come in and escort you to the Grand Hall of Tranquility. Do you have any questions?

—No, I think I am good.

—If any issues or concerns arise, we will be right outside your door waiting to assist.

— <Khogee, you still there?>

— <Yes, My Light. Of course, I am. At the same time, you mentioned an agent was announcing himself to come into your chambers, an agent was outside my door announcing he was entering my chambers. It sounds like we are headed to The Grand Hall of Tranquility to meet our parents.>

— <You mean to be reintroduced to our parents, Khogee. We have already met them. Don't you remember getting acquainted with them during our memory restoration chamber experience? We have to ensure we approach them with the same love, affection, and tenderness as the memories restored into us.>

— <Yes, of course. I will do my best. You know faking it is not my strong suit.>

— <Well, I need you to adjust and adjust quickly. The mission, and for all I know our existence here on Kashnoths, will be determined by how well the two head chiefs from the House of Khininten and Khostempain receive us. We must make them think we are fully restored to the version of us that they grew to know and love before we were sent to Isonateon.>

— <I understand, I will make sure I am 'on' and ready to perform when the time is right. Now, onto more immediately pressing matters.>

— <Yes, My Light, I am listening.>

— <How exactly do I open the doors to the closet and wash area? So, I can properly prepare myself to meet our parents.>

— <Stand in front of the closet door, look directly into your eyes reflecting back at you through the mirror. Then say your name and then the word 'open.'>

— <Wow, how did you figure that out?>

— <Oddly enough it was one of my restored memories.>

— <Interesting! Now that I have gotten what I need, I assume it closes on its own.>

— <Yes, from my most recent experience, this is correct.>

— <How interesting these clothes look just as those on Saynohs. I assumed the fashion here would be a lot different.>

— <Honestly, I am not sure what is going on. When Alcarekh advised we would be properly adorned in Kashnoths attire after entering the wash area, I expected our clothes to be something way fancier than this baggy fabric we are currently wearing. Based on the memories I had restored, the attire we wear here is a lot more sophisticated than that of Saynohs. And now they are providing us with clothes from Saynohs. I don't understand the logic behind providing us with clothes from the planet we just left. Unless it is a test. Maybe a test to confirm if we really have had our memories restored back to the versions of Khogee and Kheira, they desire us to be. When we meet our so-called parents, we must remember to make comments about how we expected to have more sophisticated Kashnoths attire for our choosing. Khogee, are you there, can you hear me?>

— <Yes, of course. I will always be here for you, My Light. I am not paying any attention to what you are saying though. However, My Light, I'm definitely here.>

— <Seriously, Khogee? This is a serious conversation! What do you mean you aren't paying attention to me? What exactly are you doing?>

— <Kheira, do you want to try something new?>

— <So, first you aren't listening to me and now you are going to ignore me like I didn't just ask you a question? What is going on with you today?>

— <Kheira, I'm going to ask you again. Do you want to try something new?>

— <Really, Khogee? Sure, we can just ignore my inquiries and focus on yours. What is it that you'd like to try?>

— <First, take all of your clothes off and look in the mirror.>

— <Wait, what?>

— <Nope, don't ask me any questions. You trust me completely, right?>

— <You know I do.>

— <Good, My Light. All I need you to do is follow my instructions. Can you do that for me?>

— <Yes, My Light, anything you ask.>

— <Let me know when you are standing in front of your mirror.>

— <I'm here now.>

— <Did you follow all the instructions, are you completely naked?>

— <Of course, My Light.>

— <Now, you know our connection goes deeper than we both understand at the current moment, right?>

— <Yes, why do you ask?>

— <Well, I have been wondering if we can recreate a similar experience to what we created on Kaytoin. You know, right before we got distracted by the assassins attempting to end us.>

— <Okay, I am following along. What do you have in mind?>

— <It isn't completely hashed out yet. But I am curious to know what we will create if we both focus our energy while looking in the mirror and simultaneously connect with one another. What will be the end result?>

— <This sounds very enticing.>

— <I'm glad you are open to experimenting.>

— <I am, but what if there truly are some sort of cameras in here?>

— <Well, I guess we will find out for sure here in a moment now, won't we?>

— <I know we only have a forty-five minute window to get ready. But if what I believe you are hoping to take place occurs, when we are done? Do you think we can go to the point in time where we still have forty-

five minutes left? This way we can ensure we don't miss our queue, or raise any suspicions.>

— <You are reading my heart, My Light. And if all else fails, they've waited for us this long, a little longer will not kill them.>

— <Let me know when you start sending me energy.>

— <Naw, My light. Let me know when you start to feel my energy. My Light, I can hear you moaning in my heart space. Kheira, speak to me. I need to hear you say you can feel me.>

— <I feel you deep inside of my soul.>

— <Open your eyes, My Light. Can you see me?>

— <Wow! Yes, I can see you. I can actually see you in the mirror approaching me from behind. Getting ready to press your stomach up against my back, and wrap your arms around me. Khogee, wait! Why can I actually feel you physically touching me?>

— <Hmmm, My Light, can you also feel me licking the left side of your neck and the fullness of me pressing into you from behind?>

— <Yes, My Light, I can! But, I don't, I don't… I don't understand how I can actually feel you touching me physically through a mirror.>

— <That's because, I am actually physically touching you, My Light. Wait, don't be afraid. Come here, turn around and look me in my eyes; allow my soul to soothe yours. I don't quite understand the science behind it. But somehow, we opened a portal through the mirrors using the power of our energy. And now I can properly consume you inch by inch, the way I've been desiring to since you walked into my school back on Saynohs.>

— <Do you think we are truly alone? What if those standing guard hear us?>

— <I thought of all those possibilities before I opened my lips with the instructions. I know it is a risk, My Light, but being here in front of you with our bodies pressed up against one another, feeling the energy of

your being wrapping me in pure light and love. This is more than worth this risk to me.>

—Kheira, is it okay for me to enter?

—No, not at this moment. I am still getting dressed.

—Okay please know you only have thirty minutes before we need to leave.

—Thank you for the time check.

—You are welcome.

— <Kheira, I can feel your trepidation. Here let's do this instead. Follow me into the wash area, and I'll gently clean you from head to toe before I return to my room and get dressed. This way we will have plenty of time to determine if we are being watched or not when we meet with our so-called parents. If the confirmation is that we are not, I will come to you again under the cover of night and let you feel the fullness of my love the way I know your entire being craves for me.>

Chapter 13:

The Show

—Khogee and Kheira, finally, we are in each other's presence again. It has been so long! Please come greet us with a warm embrace so that our energies may once again know how it feels to bask in each other's presence. I can't believe we are here with you again. Oh, how long it has been. Please sit. We have so much to speak about.

—Thank you, Mother. It is an honor for Khogee and me to grace your presence again. There has been so much time that has gone by. You have no idea how much both of us have longed to be in your presence since we were fully restored to who we are. Honestly, even though our memories were wiped, there was always a deep longing in our souls that we just couldn't quite place. How wonderful it is to have that longing quenched.

—Please sit, both of you. Now tell us, how was your journey and night's rest since you have returned.

—Yes, Mother. Our night's rest was well-needed after the long journeys we both embarked on. However, I was quite surprised at the attire we were given after going through the wash area. And even more outraged to see this grotesque Saynohs garb in my closet instead of our royal attire. Khogee looked darn right disgusted when we crossed paths on the way to the Grand Hall of tranquility.

—Oh! I am so glad to hear you say that, my daughter. We all wanted to test you and Khogee. Make sure you were truly restored to us. We hope this test did not offend either of you.

—Of course, it didn't offend me or Khogee. It is the free will of the Houses to do as they please. You can never be too careful and your safety and the safety of the Kashnoths people are always first priority.

—Yes, my dear. I am so glad you understand. I see you truly are fully your old self again.

—Do either of you have any questions for us?

—Thank you, Father, for allowing us to ask questions. I am kind of confused about a couple of things, if you don't mind entertaining a few simple questions? After our memory restoration, I understand the mission Kheira and I were sent on and its importance. However, I don't quite understand why we were trapped on Saynohs or who trapped us there. During your time of tracking us down to bring us home were you able to uncover this information?

—What an excellent question, son. We have not yet uncovered who was behind those treacherous actions as of yet. But rest assured we do have our top investigators searching for answers. While we are on this topic, I do wonder if you can help our investigation along by telling us what you do remember.

Son, look, this is perfect timing. Here is our chief science officer assisting the investigation team. Dr. Lanrete Retsam, Please come and welcome the return of your two favorite protégées!

— <Kheira, can you hear me? Here in your heart space.>

— <Khogee, you are taking a big risk speaking to me here.>

— <Trust me they are not aware of this gift.>

— <What gives you such confidence in this assessment, is it due to the simple lie your father just told you regarding them not knowing who trapped us on Saynohs? Or is it the fact that the man standing before us as their chief Scientist, is the same man as before, whose presence we just stood in front of on Isonateon? Where we knew him as our Sama.>

— <You are spot on, My Light! I love how in tune you always are with me.>

— <Yes, and if his last words to us were 'The next time you see me, do not see me! In any situation where you need my guidance, speak to me from your heart space,' then I agree your assessment is correct. They

can't know about this gift. But now I have so many questions, how is Sama here and on Isonateon, Khogee?>

— <Yes, and in the cottage. We must remember what Sama advised us though. We must not see him or let on to anyone else that we do see him.>

— <Kheira and Khogee, I am so glad the two of you remember my words. Now shall we proceed with this show of sorts?>

— <Of course, Sama. We are ready whenever you are.>

—Kheira and Khogee, I am so glad to see the two of you here before all of our eyes. We have spent so much time looking for the two of you. Can you please share with us what your experience has been since you fled Isonateon? Once we located the two of you myself and the two chief families were beside ourselves with disbelief, and completely perplexed as to how you ended up trapped in the experiment currently underway on Saynohs.

—Of course, we can. It has been an interesting journey back home for Khogee and I. When we first fled Isonateon we ended up on Kaytoin. I lost my memory completely, but Khogee had his. When an attempt was made on our lives we fled and ended up on Saynohs stuck in what seemed like a never-ending cycle of walking onstage, walking offstage, and back onstage—never remembering you'd ever been on that stage to begin with. However, this time Khogee completely lost his memories, and I retained my memories, but only up until the point where we landed on Kaytoin. I had no memory before then. Until we were rescued and brought back to our true home, where having our memories restored has made us whole.

—That is a horrible experience, Kheira. I'm so sorry the two of you had to endure this experience.

—Yes, Mother, it has been quite an ordeal getting back home. But we are truly glad to be here.

—Do either of you know who made an attempt on your life on Kaytoin?

—Honestly, no! I have no recollection of the encounter itself. Just a recollection that we had to escape Kaytoin because we were being attacked.

—So, you don't even remember how your attackers looked?

—Strangely enough, no. Mother, I do not.

—That is so odd. As your memories were fully restored, you should remember everything.

—Khogee, is this also your experience as well?

—Yes, Mother, it is.

—Hmm, we will have to chat with Aynobe to see if something is amiss.

—Now Khogee, my dear son, you said you had questions. What else did you need clarification on?

—Yes, Father, thank you for remembering and offering me the space to clear up my confusion. From what I remember, Kheira and I were sent on an undercover mission to Isonateon. However, while on Planet Isonateon there was an attack. As a result, we were made to flee and this is what inevitably put us on the path that landed us on Kaytoin and then Saynohs. Do you think the same people who constructed the attack on Kaytoin are also behind the attack on Saynohs?

—It is very possible they were sent by the same people. From what I gather based on the words you both have just spoken. Someone is hunting you down through the solar system in an effort to end your life. The more important question to me that needs further pondering is— why? If you can figure that piece of the puzzle out, I think you'll be able to see the picture clearly and know who your assailants are taking orders from. You know what, I have an idea. Have you all visited Ashbanke yet?

—Oh! What a brilliant idea! We haven't sat under Ashbanke's wisdom since we've returned. I think we will do just that once we finish our visit here. Khogee, what do you think?

—I too think Father's idea is brilliant!

—Well, what are the two of you waiting for? We are finished here and can continue to catch up later, so head over to Ashbanke right away. I am sure Ashbanke has been waiting for you two since you returned. He hasn't been the same since you left. Sitting under Ashbanke's wisdom may bring you clarity and help you put together Why any of these terrible situations have befallen the two of you.

Chapter 14:

Ashbanke

—Ashbanke, it is so good to see you, old friend.

—As it is to see you as well, Kheira and Khogee! Kheira, it has been a long while since you and Khogee's presence has glanced upon the gorgeousness of my leaves and roots, or tasted the magnificence of the best fruit in the land.

—Oh Ashbanke, how I have missed your playfulness and not so subtle boasting. May we take a seat under the shade of your leaves while we converse?

—Of course, anything for my favorite couple, but first you must greet me properly. Do you remember how?

—Well, but of course, Ashbanke. First, we will place our first eye on the center of your heart chakra, located in the same place still, I hope? Then we will hug you and bow before you, honoring all of who you are.

—Ahh Kheira, that is correct! But do you remember this on your own? Or is your remembrance only accurate due to the memories that have been restored?

—I'd not be truthful if I told you I remembered on my own.

—Interesting, how can I confirm? Let me see!

—Do you mind if I ask what it is you are attempting to confirm, Ashbanke? Are you desiring to confirm that we have been fully restored back to the Kashnoths we were before we left?

—Yes, Khogee, I am, and so much more. Answer me this if you and Kheira don't mind indulging my curiosity a little longer. How is it possible that when one closes their eyes and drifts off into sleep, they find themselves awake completely in a simulated sleep state? Just to realize they are in a reality that exists separate from the perceived reality they engage in while the eyes of their body are open filling away all that they observe. Do either of you care to take a chance at deciphering this riddle?

—Yes, Ashbanke, I will. But before I do, how do I know my words I share with you will stay only in this space and will not bounce from this ground to another's ears?

—Khogee, clever you are. I understand the state of your quandary loud and clear. Know that in the past, present, and future whenever you and Kheira step upon my ground, under my leaves, you have entered a cloaked safe space. Completely secure and free from prying ears. You truly can trust me. Please continue and provide me with your response so I can know the energy of sincere genuineness being projected from your aura and the pureness being felt from your heart is real and not a fallacy. Because the only way you can correctly answer this riddle is if you are truly tapped into the fullness of who you are before your mission on Isonateon began.

—Thank you for taking the time to reassure me of both Kheira and I's safety. My response to your riddle Ashbanke is as follows, only those who seek the truth and prove themselves worthy will truly awake to see the truth, while those who choose to accept and chase the delusion being fed to them will continue to seek and accept the illusion projected before them. Staying asleep and dreaming as they choose, never truly awakening. You quote a riddle our Sama used to say to us often on Isonateon. Ashbanke, how is this possible?

—Khogee, you tell me how you think this is possible.

—The only conclusion I can come to is that you know Sama. Still, I don't understand how that could be if you are here on Kashnoths.

—Very clever response, Khogee. I see you are still the studious observant pupil that I grew to love unconditionally. And, I think we both know the answer to that question. As I see you are ever still loyal, I will say what you sense. Yes, I know your Sama. And your Sama knows me. Yet I still haven't quite answered your question, now have I? I'd ask you how you think it is possible, but I know you are too smart to allow yourself to answer that question as you are still figuring out who to trust and are ever so cautious. In the spirit of full transparency, I'll say this. I know Sama's true origins and mission same as I know yours. I know you are thinking, 'How is that possible if you have been here on Kashnoths this entire time? And if what you are saying is true, why would he confide in you?' Let's just say that we are ancient friends, who proved their loyalty to each other, and as a result, we know we can put unequivocal trust in one another. Know that our friendship goes back before this particular solar system was ever created. And, that I'm present on every planet and timeline he currently occupies, holding space for him in whatever way needed. I can very clearly see the wheels turning in both of your minds and they are full of questions. Please ask me what you will.

—Thank you for your transparency, as I do have another question that has been pressing on my mind since Sama walked into the Great Hall of Solace. How is Sama able to move between Kashnoths and Isonateons? I would assume the Isonateons head families being former Kashnoths have to know of his role here on Kashnoths. If this assumption is true, how is it possible that the Isonateons ever trusted that he was truly loyal to them and their mission?

—An excellent question indeed, Kheira. If you will, allow me to place one of my branches on each of your first eyes. As I do, please close your eyelids, relax and allow me to show you visually what I verbalize. You see I know the two of you have acquired many missing pieces to the puzzle of you, but you still have some missing. Let me give you one of those pieces now.

The two of you originated from the same home planet. Which as you now know after your memory restoration experience is not Isonateon. However, it is also not Kashnoths. You see, your place of origin is on a planet where you know one of the creators to be the one you call Sama. Therefore, you carry the same energy signature as Sama within your soul. In other words, as he walks here on Kashnoths you are still able to recognize him in his form from Isonateon. If you see in the vision I am showing you, I'm allowing you to see his form as the Kashnoths see him.

When you see Sama, you see a six-foot-seven man with caramel sun-kissed skin, and curly white hair that hangs below his shoulders. Yet the image you see of him from the Kashnoths' perspective is that of a six-foot man, with green and yellow skin and a bald head.

—Thank you Ashbanke for providing this clarification to both of us. My mind has twisted itself in knots attempting to understand what I perceived as the most perplexing situation.

—Kheira, you are always welcome. Feel free to seek my impeccable wisdom, guidance, and knowledge whenever you find your mind twisted in knots. Now the two of you please sit, take comfort in the rays of the sun and connect with one another. Know we will have plenty of time to have further dialogue with one another. Rather it be on this planet or the next. Know always that your words are cloaked in my presence and you have the freedom to speak honestly with one another in whatever form you choose.

—Thank you, Ashbanke, for your assuredness and kindness.

Chapter 15:

Patience

— <Kheira, can you hear me here in your sacred heart space?>

— <Yes, Khogee, I can. And after Ashbanke's last comments, I'm wondering if he can as well.>

— <What is your assessment?>

— <Honestly, I'm not sure but my gut tells me we can trust Ashbanke's sincere words.>

— <Your intuition and instinct are always on point, My Light. If you trust him, so do I.>

— <Thank you, My Light. Your trust in me truly does help water the seeds of confidence sprouting in me as I reconnect to the fullness of who I am. You have no idea how much your belief in me means.>

— <Oh, I think I might have an idea. Now, my mind is spinning from everything Ashbanke just said, but I need time to process before we start dissecting the truth in his message. My Light, I have lots I have been pondering on. For starters, knowing that Kashnoths is not our true home of origin and that our so-called parents attempted to wipe all of who we are from our minds and restore only who they desire us to be concerns me. I know with all of my intuition they truly are the ones who sent assassins and agents after us to kill us! And, only when they realized their chosen course of action would not work, did they decide to bring us home.>

— <Why do you think this is?>

— <I do not know. Their actions are confusing and make no sense to me. Why stop attempting to end our existence just to bring us home, and to put on a charade? It makes no sense to me.>

— <I have been wondering the same thing, and I am glad to hear that we are both on the same page as to who we believe is truly behind the Kaytoin and Saynohs attacks. As of now, the only thing I can come up with is maybe something changed that made them feel we would be better assets to them alive rather than dead.>

— <I agree, and if you don't mind me asking, what led you to the conclusion that they are the ones behind the attempts on our lives?>

— <Like you said, why the charade? The deliberate attempt to program our mind with their version of the truth.>

— <Yes, I agree. There are so many pieces of the puzzle starting to come together for us, but yet so many more still to be uncovered. Kheira, can I ask you a more personal question?>

— <Sure, My Light.>

— <I was not sure how to bring the topic up, but this seems like the perfect time. All those lifetimes you were successful in finding me, did I always wake up to remember who I was and our true connection to one another?>

— <No. Not always. And honestly waiting for you to awaken to who you are and the depths of our bond, our trust, our love used to be very hard for me. Honestly, it was hard for me even in the lifetimes where you did. Talk about a lesson in patience.>

— <You said it 'used to be.' What changed, why did the waiting stop being so hard?>

— <Being there as long as we were, I had no choice but to find patience or I would have lost my mind. I actually remember saying to myself once, 'I feel like I am about to lose my mind.' Then my higher self says to me, 'Well you better get out of your mind and into your heart if you don't want to lose your mind.' This simple sentence started me down a path of acceptance and peace. You see, once I discovered the roots on the

tree of patience, I was able to partake of patience's fruit. Once the nourishment from the fruit completely assimilated within me, then, I was able to find beauty in allowing myself to enjoy loving you completely and unconditionally without expectations. I no longer let perceived limitations flood my mind with doubt, and negative thoughts. Thoughts that didn't serve me while I waited to see if this would be one of the lifetimes where you awakened and remembered you, remembered us.

Instead, I found the utmost beauty in patiently waiting for that moment when I felt pure joy and ecstasy-filled elation. A joy I experienced throughout each individual cell in my entire being, every time I could tell you had awakened. Simply by looking deep into your eyes and feeling the intensity of your heart while you stared back into my eyes. Searching my soul hoping to connect with the piece of me that resonates with your light. My light that fuels and increases the strength and power of light deep within your soul. In that moment, you'd feel the profoundness of the ancient bond we share that transcends time. Understand just how sincere every word, every action, and every patient-filled moment has been. Allowing you to feel in the depths of your being how unbreakable, and eternal our bond is. How pure our trust is. And, how unconditional the love we share surrounds us, constantly bathing us in light.>

— <That is beautiful, My Light. I am forever grateful to you for all the patience you have shown me.>

— <As I am to you. You have to remember our love, our bond, this impenetrable relationship we have between the two of us has spanned across this galaxy. Moving from planet to planet, and incarnation to incarnation on planet Saynohs. We have both played a multitude of different roles to one another, out of pure genuine divine love. You have played the role of the patient one to me on Kaytoin, and it was just my turn to play the role of the patient one on Saynohs. Forever, the love we each show to one another will always mirror.>

— <Kheira, I love it when you speak so poetically to me. You are truly a sight to behold, My Light.>

— <You are making me blush.>

— <Am I now? Well, come here so I can make your soul blush, My Light. Don't think I have forgotten about the date we have later tonight. I can't wait to show you and make you feel just how deep my love is for you. I promise there are no limits.>

—Khogee! Wait!

—What is it?

—Something is terribly wrong! Why does it look like you are starting to fade out of this reality?

—Stop playing, and come closer to me.

—Khogee, I am not playing. I am very serious at this moment.

—What do you mean? Everything looks the same to me. The color of your hazel brown eyes shine just as brightly as ever.

—My Light, look at your hands. Do you not see they are starting to fade out of this reality? Khogee, what is going on? Wait, Khogee! Don't go!

—Ashbanke, what is going on? How did Khogee just fade out of this reality? Where did he go?

—Something is wrong. I'm not sure what is going on but something is terribly wrong. Please, hurry and access the portal located on the right side of my trunk. You will open it the same way you greet me when you see me. Find the location that looks just like a key, and place your forehead there. The rest will be a simple remembrance for you.

—But Ashbanke, I cannot and will not leave Khogee. Where is he?

—There is no time to discuss further details. If you look to your right, you will see armed guards heading this way. I fear they are coming for you, and if they catch you, I have no idea what they will do. Someone must have figured out that you and Khogee were not quite programmed back to the versions of you they wished for you to be. Please hurry, Kheira, and move swiftly! They are picking up pace and moving fast.

—Ashbanke, thank you as always for your genuine care, love, and protection. Your concern for my safety and well-being is received with gratitude and appreciation. But I will not leave without Khogee! So let them come.

—Kheira, where do you think you are about to go!

—Mother, what is this? Why are you approaching me with armed guards?

—Drop the charades, Kheira. We know. We know all.

—Well, if you know all, then there is no point for games. Where is Khogee? If any harm comes to him, you will never have to worry about the Isonateons infiltrating this planet and destroying everything you hold dear.

—Kheira, calm down. Khogee is safe.

—If he is safe, why don't you bring him back and let him tell me himself?

—That I cannot do.

—Where exactly is he, and how did you evaporate him out of this space?

—As I said previously, Khogee is safe, so therefore we did not evaporate him. We just pulled him into another room, if you will. A backdoor to another room existing simultaneously parallel with this moment. You see, we were not one hundred percent sure if what we attempted in the memory restoration chamber worked. So, we built a fail-safe in you and Khogee's clothes. If for any reason we felt either of you were not the you we need you to be at this point in time we could separate the two of you. Simply by pulling one of you into another room in this reality. As we truly know and understand how strong and powerful the two of you are together.

—Mother, if you understand how strong we are together then you should not make the mistake of underestimating how powerful we are individually. Or how indestructible the link between us is.

—Kheira, you can say as you please to save face, but at this moment you and Khogee have been bested. Please do not put up a fight and just follow me. We have plenty of time for a question-and-answer session later.

—What exactly are your plans with me?

—To drain you dry and dissect every inch of you.

—Are these also the plans you have for Khogee?

—Of course! We will record every moment of the torture and replay it for the Kashnothian population to ensure everyone knows what happens to those who betray us. Can you envision the fear we will create within our citizens? Ending the lives of our own children for disloyalty. We will own their minds and hearts.

—Wait, what is that over there?

—Kheira, please. Do you really think I would fall for a ruse to distract me so you could attempt to flee? You must let the idea of you getting to Khogee go. The two of you will never see each other again. You have greatly underestimated us and as a result, you have ultimately caused your own demise.

—No, Mother, it is you who greatly underestimates us. If whomever it is that has Khogee makes the same mistake you have made, and tells him your plan to kill him and I. They have made a bigger mistake than the one you all made when you came up with the plan to capture us.

—Kheira, please! I see you are still delusional, thinking the two of you will ever see each other again. You will never make it off Kashnoths alive.

—Mother, you have misdiagnosed the circumstances of this situation. It is you who doesn't understand. Khogee will never let you take me, let alone harm me, and for that reason wherever you have him, you will never be able to hold him.

Chapter 16:

Truth Seeker

—Where is Kheira?

—Khogee, I have pulled you through a backdoor from the moment in time you were just in to another room existing alongside the moment in time you were just in. And, all you seem to be worried about is Kheira. No concern for your own life at all? How foolish of you.

—Father, please save the mental games for someone else. The only concern I have at this moment is the location of Kheira. Is Kheira safe?

—She is exactly where you left her. I would say she is safe and free from harm, but I might be lying to you. You see, I know what plans I have for you so I can only imagine the plans her mother has for her.

—So, if I understand you correctly you are telling me that Kheira is not safe, correct?

—Yes, of course, that is what I am saying to you. But you need to forget about her and understand that you are not safe and that is all you should be concerned about. Kheira is gone, completely out of reach from you. You will never see her again. Come to terms with your new reality in this moment and focus on your own well-being.

—If this is the case, it doesn't sound like you all have plans for either of us to make it off of this planet alive, correct?

—Yes, Khogee, you are finally starting to see the bigger picture at play here.

—Well, since your personal plans do not include me walking out of this room, would you mind indulging me by simply answering a few short questions before you start your torture and interrogation session?

—Usually, I would decline such a request. But for you, I'd be glad to. What is it that you'd like to know?

—First of all, why would you torture your own kids this way, who is it that you believe we are?

—Really? Of all the questions you could have asked, this is the question you have?

—Khogee, I raised you with all the love I have to give, and for that reason and that reason alone, in my heart, you will always be my son. However, I know in the mechanics of my mind, based on what we have discovered, there is no way you could truly be my son. We know the memory restoration chamber did not work on you in the manner we had hoped. The both of you have become soft, no longer desiring to conquer and reign supreme by any means necessary.

—How exactly did you know we weren't back to the version of us you desired?

—Honestly, we all wanted to believe the memory restoration chamber would be able to restore you back to your full Kashnothian versions. Yet we all knew there was a greater possibility the restoration wouldn't work than there was that it would work. Still, I have yet to answer your question. See, you all passed every single test we placed before you. Recognizing the clothes from Saynohs in your closet are not the proper attire you normally adorn your bodies with while here on Kashnoths. The both of you remembering the proper greeting and showing proper etiquette through dinner. Everything was perfect! We were all so overjoyed thinking the restoration chamber had truly worked, rejoicing in the fact we had the two of you back.

—I don't quite understand. If we did everything as perfect as you say, what made you all come to the assumption we aren't us, and when did you truly start to suspect?

—Honestly, our concern started when your transport to Isonateon went wrong. When you ended up in the fetus versus the toddler. We did not know for sure but felt it was possible the full memories of who you were and the details of your full mission may have been lost. We knew for sure that our concerns were valid when we came to rescue the both of you, but you fled. However, we had hope as you recognized your true names when called Kheira and Khogee, and not the names you were called on Isonateon. You know Lanrete Retsam named the two of you while you were still in the wombs of Madam Khostempain and Khininten. Anyway, enough of this sentimental, back to the point. The two of you had no true idea of who you were, all you remembered was Isonateon as your home source. So, we knew you didn't remember when you left Kashnoths for your mission on Isonateon that the blueprint of your energy signature was attuned to a specific technology we have since transferred to the Way Finder. The attuning and connection formed as a result allowed us to track your soul's signature any and everywhere. This is how we have always known where you were.

As far as us being able to tell the memory restoration chamber did not work, well it surely wasn't how you all maneuvered the Kashnoths culture that gave you away. You see we know the two of you are the best of the best and excel in the art of being chameleons. To ensure you would not be able to fool us we had the science lab create the Truth Seeker. The Truth Seeker took time to develop. So, your deciding to take the both of you to Kaytoin to regroup gave us the perfect window of time. However, while on Kaytoin we observed the two of you, and we noticed the two of you were tapping into and displaying gifts that the Kashnoths and Isonateons do not possess. None of us fly, son. None of us! I noticed that Kheira had lost all her memory but you had not. Even more, you started to pull in deeper memories from the recesses of your soul. Memories that do not belong to Isonateon or Kashnoths. I believe in your head you thought these memories belonged to what you believed at the time was your home of origin, Isonateon.

I was blinded by my love for you, my son. I rationalized what I was seeing with the fact that you and Kheira have always been special and the most gifted of our people. That you were tapping into ancient gifts of our people long forgotten. And yet, still something always felt off. I was not the only one who felt something was off. Unbeknownst to myself or Lord Khininten, your mothers sent assassins to end your lives. They felt that you were imposters. That their children had been killed and replaced. Lord Khininten and myself were able to persuade them to no longer pursue their current course of action and give us time to come up with an alternative plan. This is why you were stranded on Saynohs for so long. We needed time to allow our strongest scientists to create the Truth Seeker. However, as we watched you and Kheira moving in and out of so many characters, we found it very odd that every time you were on the brink of actually awakening and discovering who you are, you were somehow killed.

—Wait, that wasn't you all?

—No, it wasn't. Our plan was to let you all stay there exit out naturally and then cycle back in. There was no way for you to escape Saynohs without our help. Why would we intentionally keep killing you?

—How do you know it wasn't our mothers?

—We helped them realize you were truly still our kids and had pulled in ancient gifts from those who walked Kashnoths before us. Their faith in us, and you being stranded on Saynohs, allowed us time to create a device that would tell us the truth of who you are. Once developed, we would use the memory restoration chamber to restore your files back to what they were before you left Kashnoths and then we could use the Truth Seeker to be sure you are truly ours.

Now, this is where the Truth Seeker comes into play. The Truth Seeker is able to read energy fields around the heart and interpret this energy in a myriad of ways. The energy can be interpreted into colors, mathematical equations, as well as geometrical shapes. The colors let us know the intentions of a person. The mathematical equations let us know the true origins of a person and the geometrical shapes come together in patterns that let us know if we are in the midst of a spy, assassin, or an ally. While we all conversed in the Great Hall of Solace, we had two of our finest scientists scan both of you with the Truth Seeker from the far-right corner of the room. This vantage point was best because no matter how brilliant the two of you are, you don't seem to have eyes in the back of your head. We enticed the two of you to spend time with Ashbanke so we could analyze the data properly. And oh, how interesting the reports were on both of you. In the colors, we saw your intentions are pure, no harm to us do you desire to bring. You two truly do have pure hearts. However, the mathematical equations were not able to determine your true point of origin. This was the first red flag, and honestly, the only one we needed. But we were at an even greater loss when the geometrical shapes were unable to produce any patterns that could be interpreted. The reading was quite baffling to our top scientist. As the Truth Seeker has the location of every planet in this galaxy mapped within its equations. It turns out this entire time we do not know who it is we have perceived to be our children. So, Khogee, my question for you is, what are you and Kheira's place of origin and what exactly are the two of you?

—This is unfortunately a question that I cannot answer for you, Father.

—Come now, Khogee. At this point, you can stop calling me father. The truth has been laid out plainly and clearly. We both know I am not your father! And I will forever be perplexed in my attempts to figure out how you were created by my DNA but are not from Kashnoths. Anyway, I will move past the heartache I feel deeply in my soul at some point. As I can always produce another heir. It is time for us to move forward with the reason I brought you here. Is there anything else you'd like to ask before we begin?

—Yes, there is. When will I be allowed to see Kheira?

—Khogee, we have already discussed this, and I thought you understood what was truly going on here. So let me say this for the last time, do your best to let the truth sink in. You will never see Kheira again! Our plan is to drain all the light from you both, and completely dissect you until there is nothing left. We need to understand who and what you are, and if we can replicate such unique creatures. But first, you will answer my question regarding where you are from and who you are.

—Father, are you saying to me when you made the previous statement, 'you could only imagine the plans her mother has for her' you were actually speaking fact?

—Yes, Khogee, that is correct.

—And, to be sure that I understand you correctly, the intention of the Kashnoths is to kill both Kheira and myself?

—Yes, what about my previous statements allows this to be a question in your mind?

—I had to make sure before I move forward with my next steps. You see, if you had said it was me you were after and Kheira could go if I sacrificed myself, I might have been able to let you live, but I will never allow you to bring harm to Kheira. For this reason alone, I must do what must be done. The energy and light within me and all around us are mine to wield. As I have been on Kashnoths long enough to know that you have not yet mastered yourselves or learned how to harness the power from within. You are too busy seeking to gain power by conquering that which is outside of you.

—Khogee, please. Let go of your pride. There is no way for you to break free of the stone-reinforced metal chains we have bound you in. If you will not admit defeat to me, at least admit it to yourself.

—Father, I did seek permission to ask a few questions. May I now proceed with my next one?

—Of course, I will indulge one more.

—You stated earlier that Kheira is in another room. How exactly did you go about separating us into two side-by-side realities? Kheira stated she noticed I was fading away, however, she never mentioned that she saw me going through a portal of any sort.

—Now, Khogee, this is a question. A question truly worthy of a response. While the scientists were inventing the Truth Seeker, they also invented another nifty gadget called the Way Finder. You see, the Way Finder is lined all throughout you and Kheira's clothes. It is untraceable and weighs nothing. You never even knew it was there. This particular gadget is what allowed us to pull you into this parallel reality created specifically for us to house and do as we will with our enemies. For anyone who does not stand with us is against us.

—How exactly does the gadget work?

—Khogee, we do not have time to get into the nuts and bolts of this unparalleled scientific achievement. What I will say is this diamond-crusted ring you see on my index finger is what allows me control over the part of the Way Finder that is in your clothes. And Kheira's mother has the other ring that gives her control of the part of the Way Finder in

Kheira's clothes. Originally the plan was to pull Kheira into this parallel reality, but we decided it would be better to pull you here instead.

—Why exactly did you all feel it would be better to pull me here instead of Kheira?

—Figured it would be easier to keep you contained here without any weapons easily at your disposal.

—And you think it is safe to keep Kheira where weapons are at her disposal? You are right in your assessment of not truly knowing who we are. Is there no way to get you all to reconsider your plans to harm Kheira?

—Khogee, again, why the focus on Kheira when it is your own life you should be concerned about? In this moment you are proving just how soft you have become, and this softness you have required is going to be your downfall.

—No, Father. It is the brightness of My Light's love that allows me to dive deep into the depths of my own light, strengthening me from the inside out. Father, it is my softness, as you call it, that empowers me. However, it will be your arrogance, lack of true sight, and unwillingness to have true knowledge of self that will cause your downfall sooner than you realize.

Chapter 17:

Good-Bye

—Madam Khininten, I'm not sure what is going on but Kheira is right, look there behind you. Do you see as we see? Swirls of light are starting to form with lighting shooting all around.

—General Tathanboth, I'm not sure what is going on, but I'm confident there is nothing to be alarmed about… Oh my goodness! This can't be! Khogee, how did you escape and get back here?

—Kheira, are you okay?

—Yes, no harm has come to me. You are always right on time, My Light.

—The two of you are not going anywhere. I'm not sure how you escaped, Khogee, but there is no way you are getting off this planet.

—Try and stop us, Mother.

—Have you both been gone so long that you have become delusional? There is no way the two of you can defeat our entire army.

—Mother, we don't have to defeat your army, just you.

—Stand back Madam Khininten, get behind us.

—General Tathanboth, I will do no such thing. I'm perfectly fine. Any second now Lord Khostempain will present himself from the side-by-side reality with the other half of our personal army, and we will proceed forward with our plans.

—Actually, he will not be joining us in a second or any time after for that matter.

—Khogee, what have you done?

—I have done what any warrior does when his life and that of his love is being threatened. Now please let Kheira go and we will leave this planet, Madam Khininten.

—You can't tell me that you defeated him when he had over five hundred armed personnel with him. This is not possible.

—Anything and everything is possible. You should never underestimate this truth or your perceived enemy. Now, please let Kheira go so we do not have to experience any further bloodshed on this day.

—You are bluffing. There is no way you took your own father's life.

—Madam Khininten, how is it that you cannot allow yourself to conceive this possibility when his own aim was to end my life first? Again, I ask sincerely that you let Kheira come to me so we can exit this planet.

—We will never let you leave, and whatever game you are playing at will not work. Your father will be here shortly, but his personal army is not needed. My personal army that I have here of five hundred will be enough to apprehend the two of you so we can move forward with our plans.

—Here, would the ring he used for the Way Finder and the finger it was attached to be enough proof to show you that I am not playing games as you say?

—Oh, my goodness! General Tathanboth, take them both into custody immediately.

—With honor, madam.

—Khogee, before I have General Tathanboth take you into custody, I need you to tell me how you on your own defeated Lord Khostempain, and his personal army of five hundred.

—If you would like to move forward with your intended course of action, I can show you better than I can tell you.

—General Tathanboth, what are you doing?

—Madam Khininten, I am letting Kheira go so that she and Khogee can leave this planet.

—Why would you defy my orders, General Tathanboth?

—Madam Khininten, do you see that gold and emerald star-shaped amulet hanging around Khogee's neck?

—Yes, of course. Well, that belonged to the admiral, and he never took it off. If Khogee now adorns his most sacred artifact then there is much more at play in this moment than we are aware of. Do you want us to move into an unknown situation where you could potentially lose the only five hundred remaining men and women assigned specifically for your defense? You say you doubt his ability to have taken down half the royals' personal army along with his father, Lord Khostempain. Yet you expect myself and the rest of your personal army to overlook the fact you and his father, Lord Khostempain needed all of your personal army to apprehend just two people. There is much more at play indeed. I will not put more lives at stake when it is clear you all are not telling us the full story as to who these two truly are or what these two are truly capable of. Proper reconnaissance needs to be completed and we need a better understanding of who and what we are up against. For all I know Khogee has an entire army waiting to come through via the Way Finder to end all of our lives and tear Kashnoths to shreds. Is this a chance you are willing to take?

—Madam Khininten, if I were you, I'd consider the general's words very clearly. And make sure your next move is based on sound intuition and not the rashness of pride.

—Even if we let you and Kheira go there is no way for the two of you to leave this planet.

—Madam Khininten, you forget I have the other key to the Way Finder. Now please take off your key and give it to Kheira. As we leave, please do not follow us.

Chapter 18:

Escape

—Khogee, I knew you would come back for me.

—Always, My Light. My only concern was getting back to you.

—Even in times of your own peril you still put me first.

—Into eternity, My Light.

—I have been curious, how exactly did you escape? And do you have a plan for us to truly get off this planet? Us being in this separate room within this reality is not the same as us getting off this planet. A plan is surely being cooked up at this very moment on the best way to infiltrate this space and take us out.

—I will tell you everything, My Light, but first we must rid ourselves of these clothes. Based on what Lord Khostempain advised me, they have the ability to transport us to whatever location they wish as long as we have on these clothes—with technology they created called the Way Finder.

—Great thinking, My Light. Now that we are free of our tracking devices, tell me what happened.

—Well, before I do that, we technically aren't completely free of all our tracking devices. There is one more tracking device that I need to deactivate. I will need you to trust me and stay very still, this will not hurt but may cause you to be unbalanced for a few minutes when I am done. To ensure they could keep up with us across the solar system they tuned the blueprint of our essence to a certain frequency that could only be detected by their technology. Once the Way Finder was invented, they were able to transfer the technology to the rings their chief scientists created to be extensions of the Way Finder. As a result, I now have the ability to remove this frequency from your blueprint. So even if they have a backup Way Finder, they will never be able to track us down.

—Khogee, look at this orange dust coming out of my hands. I am curious if this dust-like energy field is what allowed them to track our soul signatures down throughout time.

—That is a great deduction, My Light. Here take this ring and remove the tracker from me, let's see if the results are the same. Wow, My Light, I believe you are on to something. Look at all the orange dust-like energy coming out of my hands. This orange dust-like energy looks the exact same as what just came out of your hands. Now I am curious as to how they got this in our essence and how it stayed attached to us for so long.

—Maybe they grafted it onto our energy somehow. And with the Kashnoths magic, they were able to engineer it in a way where it attaches to the soul essence in the body.

—This is a good theory. Now that we have this orange dust-like energy tracker out of us we need to ensure we never again give them the opportunity to put this tracker back in us. To answer your question about what happened, Kheira. My father used the Way Finder to pull me into this mirror reality. I asked him a few questions to better understand how they knew we weren't the versions of them they needed us to be; as well as how he pulled me into another reality. He then explained to me their plans for you and I, and those plans did not end with either of us leaving this planet alive. After he answered the rest of my questions, he proceeded to take me to a machine they call The Deconstructor. This is where your mother was also about to escort you. Once there, they laid me on a table with the plans to start draining the light from me and proceed with dissecting my body.

—I am so curious as to how one drains light from another.

—I am too, My Light, but I was not curious enough to be the test subject for their new experiment. When they escorted me into the room where The Deconstructor resides, I immediately felt an intense amount of energy radiating from the device. So I allowed them to move forward with their plans. This way they could remain under the delusion they were the ones who held all the power, and I would have more time to harness the energy from The Deconstructor. Lying on the table, I was able to pull in enough energy from this machine in order to amplify my strength and stamina. I was able to break free of the restraints they bound me with and from there make quick work of my father and the six armed guards in the room with us, including the admiral.

—Quick thinking on your part to grab the admiral's amulet and your father's finger as proof they had been defeated.

—Thank you, but there is one thing I must tell you.

—I am all ears, My Light.

—Well, the rest of the armed guards are still here as I did not defeat the entire army. My only focus was getting back to you as quickly as I could. I did not track the rest of the guards down to take them out before I came for you.

—So you are saying there are armed guards walking around here in this reality looking for us.

—Yes and no. They are here but they are not walking around looking for us. I heard the admiral dismiss them before we headed to The Deconstructor. I'm not sure where he dismissed them too. They could be back on Kashnoths or here in this other reality. We must be careful in our movements and alert at all times until we figure out how to get out of here.

—What I'm hearing is that we need a plan.

—Yes, My Light we do. Do you have any thoughts?

—As you stated earlier, this back room you brought us to is a mirror of the reality we were just in. If this is truly the case, it should mimic the Kashnoths home planet. And if this is a true mirror of where the Kashnoths reside, I wonder if Ashbanke is here as well. Let us see if we can find him. There is a portal we can access hidden within him to take us to safety.

—That is a great idea. You lead the way, Kheira. I will be right behind you.

—Yes, Ashbanke! You have no idea how thankful I am that you are here.

—Khogee and Kheira, I am glad to see you both. Wonderful escape the two of you made back there. I'm assuming the two of you need my assistance with getting off of this planet.

—Yes. Yes, we do. Is the offer to use your portal for escape still on the table?

—Yes, Kheira, of course. Anything for my two favorite people on this planet. You know where the door is and how to access it. But before you do, is the intention for the two of you to walk through the portal naked?

—Oh yes, we need clothes, Khogee. Yeah, I was so caught up in our plan of escape I forgot we were naked. I would say we could go get some from one of the rooms we slept in last night. But honestly, I do not trust that they are not also filled with trackers.

—I agree with your assessment, Kheira. So, Yes, Ashbanke we will be walking through naked.

—I'm disappointed in you two. You stand before the Grand, Great, and Powerful Ashbanke, who has a portal hidden within him and do not have enough thought of me to believe that I can also conjure. I see your visions aren't big enough just yet. Wait here one moment, patiently. I will make you something from my leaves. Since you didn't recognize my might and power, I will need you two to turn around and close your eyes. You don't deserve to see my magnificence.

—Ashbanke, do not be like that. You know we are in war mode. We never meant to underestimate your amazing abilities.

—That may be the case, Kheira, but you are both still in time out. Now please turn around. Okay, the two of you can open your eyes now.

—Wow, Ashbanke. You made us color-coordinated outfits. Mine is very sleek, form-fitting, and does not hinder any of my movements. Thank you again, Ashbanke.

—You are very welcome, my dear.

—Now the two of you make sure you take great care of these garments, as they will be the most amazing clothes you will ever own. I know the two of you would love to bask in the brilliance of my presence all day, but it is time for you to leave. Remember what I have told you before. I am on every planet as the one to whom you call Sama. So, this is not goodbye, but a see you soon.

—Thank you Ashbanke for always being here for us and for providing us with a safe passage off of this planet. We are eternally grateful to you.

Chapter 19:

Where Are We?

—Khogee and Kheira, it is nice to see you all again.

—Sama, what a pleasant surprise to find you here. And, speaking of here, where exactly are we?

—Kheira, you both have entered a transient way station with doorways to many dimensions and worlds. Your next destination awaits the two of you.

—Sama, do you have any guidance you can offer us on where we should go next? Our cover has been blown on Kashnoths, which means we are not safe on any of the planets we have been on since we originally left Kashnoths. But, honestly, I'm not sure if we will be safe anywhere the Kashnoths can reach.

—Khogee and Kheira, do not overly concern yourselves with where you should go next. War is coming, and your service is still needed elsewhere. Before we get to the next leg of your mission, I know you both do not have your full memories restored. Come forth with me. I will make you both chairs out of the stardust; this way you can sit in a relaxed state while I bring all of your files fully back online.

—Thank you, Sama! This is truly beyond my expectations. Kheira and I are eternally grateful to you for your kindness. How long will the entire process take?

—No more questions from either of you. As I start the process the two of you will leave your bodies and see the files most important to your overall mission in real time. The other files will be there for you to access anytime you need. Are you both ready?

—Yes, we are!

—Just close your eyes and enjoy the ride. The two of you are all finished. How do you feel?

—I feel complete and whole, like I've reconnected to the fullness of who I am.

—That's wonderful, Kheira. Now how about you, Khogee?

—The same as what Kheira stated, I also feel really strong at a soul and physical level.

—This is wonderful news. I rarely bring all files back online for anyone as it could cause a mental break if the mind isn't ready. However, I could see in both of your energy fields that you could handle the process and transitions. Your words are a wonderful confirmation. Now let us discuss your next steps. I need you both to go to the Eclanite world to assist with an impending invasion.

—Eclanite, Sama? Aren't they the people that previously owned Saynohs?

—Yes, that is correct, Kheira.

—Why would we help them, Sama? What they have done to the people on Saynohs is horrendous.

—Kheira, you tell me why we would help the Eclanite people. Your files are back online, you should know this answer yourself. Close your eyes, breathe deeply and access the file that holds the data of the memory you need. There you go, Kheira. Can you see?

—Yes, Sama, I can. The Eclanites are actually our allies. The memories previously restored from the Kashnoths' royal families were misconstrued for the purpose of deception. The Eclanites aren't the ones who enslaved the Saynohs population. They just recently took over as owners of Saynohs and were working on a plan to assist the Saynohs people with ending the seemingly never-ending cycles they are stuck in. However, Kashnoths Imperial Royal Council made a decision to take over this planet as part of their expansion program. Or 'total domination' program is the title I prefer. We need to go help the Eclanites. The Kashnoths Imperial Royal Council is afraid of retaliation from the

Eclanite's and as a result, the Kashnoths plan to destroy the Eclanite population. This is horrible, how can a group of people be so evil? Khogee and I are ready to serve and assist in any way needed, Sama. Something must be done to put Kashnoths' plan to a stop once and for all.

—Your loyalty and willingness to always be of sacrifice has never gone unnoticed. I will point you all to the correct door to take in order to safely be received by the Eclanites. Before you leave, take special note of what I am about to say. You will both be in your true bodies, the forms you both most intimately know each other in. Do not be alarmed when you gaze upon yourself or each other. You are both back in the fullness of your power which means the connection the two of you share will be felt more intensely than the two of you have felt in a very long time. Always remember your training. If the energy between the two of you becomes overwhelmingly intense, remember to channel your energy through your chakra paths. Remember your mission comes first, but you should enjoy the depths of your bond. Your connection and bond will help fuel your souls as you move ahead on the next stage of your journey. Rely on one another, stay focused, and remember loyalty is always required.

Chapter 20:

Reunion

—Khogee, My Light. Look at your skin. Wow! Look at my skin. We look magnificent. This is the exact complexion I saw of our skin when I visited the water cottage in my dream back on Kaytoin.

—Yes, Kheira, I remember you describing this particular nightly travel to me.

—Wow, being back in the form we resonate with the most feels absolutely breathtaking and complete.

—Yes, Kheira. I agree.

—Now based on the download Sama put into our consciousness before we left, we are looking for our guide, Seema. From the download I can see in my first eye, Seema is purple with long green hair down her back that she usually wears in one long thick braid. She is very stealthy, always ready to practice her skills on an unexpecting target so stay on guard. Seema and her pair, Dima, are both dear friends of ours.

—Kheira, my recollection aligns with yours.

—That is good news, Khogee, we are back, and I can't wait to see Seema and Dima again.

—Ah, Kheira, you remember me.

—Seema! Where did you come from? I didn't hear or sense you anywhere around us.

—Well, you see. I have mastered a new form of magic. This particular magic is the highest achievement of our chief shaman. Recently Shemindsonlyone was visiting amongst the ancestors during the first moon of Kwan Yin in the fifth consecutive season of mastering compassion within our inner verse. While Shemindsonlyone visited beyond the veil, she was allowed to go before the ancestors that make up the Eclanite Council of Sacred Magic. The magic practiced by this council has not been passed down through our lineage for some time. Times before time's past, the elder chief clansman, shaman, and the head of our people used this sacred magic for personal gain, the Council of Sacred Magic decided it was to be removed from our people until we were able to evolve our hearts back to the place of compassion and purity they originated from. It has taken a new elder chief clansman and a new shaman, and the head of our people, but most importantly time to get to where we are now. Once the Council of Sacred Magic saw our progression and deemed us worthy, they approved select members of the Eclanite people to regain knowledge of our people's sacred magic. Finally, we are on the right path, as enough of our hearts have become purified and deemed worthy.

However, I know after all of that talking I still have not answered your question. Honestly, I have been here this entire time. I received a message from Sama not too long ago letting me know that the two of you would be returning to assist us in battle. I have been at the portal door you all came through waiting, invisible to the naked eye, the unseen eye or the intuitive senses of those completely tapped into their core. The magic of my people is powerful! This will even the battle between the Kashnoths who defeated my people previously.

Now, please follow me. I will escort you both over to our estate. I have prepared the guest house to accommodate your stay. I hope it is worthy of your presence. Dima will be so excited to spend time with you again, Khogee. He is at our estate now preparing a meal fit for a queen and king. I know that you two have traveled far and been through a treacherous journey to arrive here at our aid. We will discuss our battle plans in depth tomorrow, but tonight the four of us will enjoy each other's company and reminisce with old stories of battle. Like the time Kheira and I had to save you and Dima from a pack of wolves deep in the Trivarious mountains located on the south side of Eclanite.

—Wow, Seema really? I thought after telling that story a million times you would have found a new one to tell.

—Oh no, Khogee, I will never ever tire of telling this story. The sheer delight and excitement both of you had when you saw us coming to your rescue. The story of the pack of wolves deep in the Trivarious mountains must live on forever. Let's finish the story in Dima's presence so you both can simultaneously acknowledge that Kheira and I are better warriors than you both.

—Seema, what foolishness is it that I hear you speak of. Now you know Khogee and I will never acknowledge such untruths.

—Dima, My Heart, did you tire of waiting for us?

—Never, My Heart, I would wait at the ends of the world for you until time ceased to exist and it still wouldn't be too long.

—Kheira and I thought you and I did too much.

—Khogee, my brother, embrace me. It has been quite a while since we have been able to embrace peace in one another's energy.

—Yes, my brother, too long it has been, indeed. I'm so grateful to be here in your energy field once again.

—Now, I am sure our guests are hungry. Let's speed up this adventure and teleport to the kitchen, Seema.

—What is it that you have cooking over here? The aroma is very tantalizing.

—Brother, come over and taste the best meal you will find on Eclanite. The secret is that I cook everything over a wood fire. It adds a unique flavor that can't be duplicated by any other cooking method. That, and there is no stronger ingredient than love.

—How exactly do you get the ingredient of love into the food, Dima?

—Kheira, I am so happy that you have asked. It is a special family secret I cannot share, but let's just say it is all in the hands.

—Are the two of you ready for me to finish the story of how Kheira and I saved your lives on the Trivarious mountains?

—Seema, I could hear this story fifty million times and would never lose interest in it at all.

—Yes, it's nice to have someone around who appreciates the art form of storytelling. Now, where was I?

—Well, I think you should start from the beginning in case Khogee and Dima forgot any details.

—Yes, Kheira, great thinking as always. As my memory serves me, I remember you and I were walking in a field bathing ourselves in the beautiful pink and purple hues of the sunrise. Then we both heard an extremely loud growling and snarling coming from every direction. However, we looked around and saw nothing. That is when I felt you in my soul, Dima, while Kheira felt Khogee at the same time. We merged with the two of you and assessed the situation through your eyes. Being the stealth warriors that we are, we instantly teleported to your location where we found the two of you holding one another shivering in fear. In unison Kheira and I...

—Seema, Khogee, and I were holding each other shivering in fear? Are you serious?

—Dima, do I interrupt you while you are in the zone of your craft? No. No, I do not. So please do not interrupt me while I'm in the zone of my craft. Thank you. Now where was I? Yes. In unison, Kheira and I grabbed hands and connected with the pack's hive mind, calming them and letting them know there was no danger and nothing to fear. Once they felt the pureness of our energy, they bowed their heads in acknowledgment of what I assume is our awesome greatness. Then they turned and left.

—Seema every time you tell this story it seems like I hear new details. The part about us holding one another and shivering in fear is quite hilarious.

—See, Dima? Khogee can appreciate and respect the art of great storytelling. Dima, My Heart, you should definitely take some notes.

—I am, My Heart. What I have so far is how important it is to respond in a way that flatters you without you realizing that I'm patronizing you at the same time. Great technique there, Khogee. I see you, my brother.

—Oh, my goodness, how I have missed the fun banter we enjoy between the four of us.

—I know it's been a while since we have seen each other, but with the impending war on the horizon, I feel we should get down to business immediately. Khogee and Kheira, I believe we should brief both of you on the plan before we visit with the chief warrior and her council tomorrow.

—Dima, are we not able to have this conversation tomorrow? Let us have this night to enjoy as we do not know when we will have this opportunity again.

—Seema, My Heart, I understand your desire. Feel my heart and know the depth of my intentions. This is not a conversation we should put off until tomorrow. Things are so volatile right now—we need to be prepared for anything and at any time. As we do not know when the battle may begin.

—Pardon my interruption, Dima. I feel you and I do understand, My Heart. Please continue.

—Grab your plates, everyone, and we will eat outside around the fire pit, and enjoy the meal I have prepared under the gloriousness of the shimmering stars while we bring the two of you up to speed.

Chapter 21:

Shemindsonlyone

—Shemindsonlyone has fought beside your Sama in many battles. She was actually chosen by him to come here and lead the Eclanite warrior clans as he has had her do on other worlds before this one.

—Yes, Dima I do have this memory in my files. Kheira and I have had the great pleasure of being trained by Shemindsonlyone on the planet Isonateon. There she was known as Theonewhoquestions. Her skin was mustard green with pink purple locks flowing down her back.

—Kheira and Khogee, I knew I felt your very uniquely distinct energy signature here on Eclanite.

—Theonewhoquestions, it is an honor and privilege to be in your presence again. I apologize, do you prefer us to call you Shemindsonlyone here on this world?

—Yes, Khogee that would be best as it will cause less confusion. Thank you for the respect you pay me through your deep bows. I too am privileged and honored to be in the presence of my four best pupils. I know you all were not expecting me here at the present moment. However, there has been a new finding that has required me to change our previous plan of meeting on tomorrow's eve. Seema, I hear the wandering in your mind. And until you and Kheira spar against Dima and Khogee in an official capacity, you can't claim that you and Kheira are the best out of the four of you.

—My deepest apologies, Shemindsonlyone.

—Really, Seema!

—Sorry, My Heart. You know how my mind wanders.

—Let us focus and get back to the reason why I have come to you all earlier than our intended meeting tomorrow. As the four of you know there is an attack on the horizon. However, this attack is more imminent than we previously realized. Earlier today while in his garden our chief seer, Mohaneace, saw in his first eye warships surrounding the Eclanite world. The vision was a shock to Mohaneace, but what shocked him the most about the vision was not the Eclanite world being surrounded by warships. What caught him off guard and disturbed him, was seeing the five of us beyond the veil setting before the Eclanite Council of Sacred Magic. It was in this moment, while we were sequestered behind the veil, that the Kashnoths struck. The head of the Eclanite Council of Sacred Magic stopped the meeting and advised us that we needed to return immediately to assist with the battle. There was just one problem. For some reason, we were not able to get back onto this side of the veil. Seema and Dima, your world was lost as a result. Our presence at this battle is paramount. The sections of the warrior clans that each of you leads need your presence, light, and guidance to help strengthen their resolve. Without our presence and combined power, the Kashnoths will destroy the Eclanite world. What is even more alarming about this vision is that I actually intended on taking the four of you before the Eclanite Council of Sacred Magic on tomorrow's eve. Shortly after we sat amongst the Eclanite Chief Warrior Council.

—Shemindsonlyone, if you don't mind, who else knew about your plans to take the four of us before the Eclanite Council of Sacred Magic?

—The only ones who knew were the members of the Eclanite Chief Warrior Council which is made up of all the Chief Clansmen. There is no one else I would trust with this information. I see where you are going in your thought process, Khogee, and my thoughts are the same.

—Yes, Shemindsonlyone, there is a disloyal amongst the ranks of the Eclanite Chief Warrior Council.

—Yes, there is Khogee, and I am most humbled and thankful the Eclanite Council of Sacred Magic provided our chief seer with this vision so he could warn me of the treachery in our midst.

—With this newfound information at hand, and you showing up here outside of your originally scheduled meeting time with us, you must have a new plan.

—Yes, Seema, that is correct. We are going to see the Eclanite Council of Sacred Magic now.

—Please forgive me if the following question is disrespectful, as it is not my intention to insult you at all. Who else knows about you coming to us tonight other than the chief seer?

—Kheira, your question is not disrespectful at all. Instead, it shows me you and Khogee both have not lost a step since the last time our presence graced one another. As I too was concerned that the chief seer may be planting information in my mind to influence the steps I chose to take next. So, I in turn planted information as well. I advised the chief seer that I was very thankful for him sharing this extremely important message with me and to share it with no one else. I then let him know that we would not visit the Eclanite Council of Sacred Magic until two days after our intended visit. We would leave the presence of the Chief Warrior Council after our regularly scheduled meeting tomorrow and instead of going before the Eclanite Council of Sacred Magic, we will hide out in a secret location. This way we will be lying in wait for the attack. Completely unbeknownst to the Kashnoths or the Eclanite Chief Warrior Council. As long as the betrayal is not deeper than it currently seems to be, the Kashnoths will continue along their intended course of action as planned.

—Thank you for answering my question, Shemindsonlyone. This is a smart plan. If for any reason the attack is postponed two days during the exact time you advised the chief seer we will be behind the veil; you will then know the poison from the members of the Eclanite Chief Warrior Council has spread.

—Do you all agree with this plan?

—Shemindsonlyone, it sounds like an excellent plan. However, I can't say that I know for sure the plan is an excellent one until I understand your reason for taking us before the Eclanite Council of Sacred Magic.

—Again, I say to you all, I too am privileged and honored to be in the presence of my star pupils. Your keen observation will forever be a catalyst that will place you ahead of all those who dare to cross your path with any intention of harm. Khogee, this is the correct question to ask. My goal in taking the four of you before the Eclanite Council of Sacred Magic is to have you all blessed, and for them to pour the golden light which they yield into your heart space and surround your body with the pink light they bestow upon those pure of heart. The pink light will serve as an additional protection barrier for you and increase your compassion which in turn will increase your strength. The golden light will increase your power, sharpen all of your senses, and increase the golden light chord that you share between one another, Kheira and Khogee. As well as deepen the connection you share with one another, Seema and Dima. This will make the four of you unbeatable against the Kashnoths army. The pink and golden light are undetectable, even to the best seer.

—Yes, Seema, your thoughts are correct. I have been bestowed with these same gifts and they have made me a stronger, more efficient warrior. Unbeatable to all who make the mistake of crossing my path with the intention to do harm. Are there any more questions before we prepare for our journey?

—Yes, can you tell us more about the Chief Warrior Council?

—Of course, Khogee. What are you hoping to gain from this information?

—A better understanding of the power our potential disloyal or disloyals wield.

—Well, there are five Chief Clansmen. Each leads a clan and each member of the clan wields the sacred Eclanite magic. Each chief and clan member also has been trained to battle and are very skilled warriors. In addition to wielding the sacred Eclanite magic and being skilled warriors, each clan has a very specific ability the other clans do not have.

The Clan That Knows No Fear, as their name states, literally does not have any fear. This may seem like a small gift. But, because fear does not register in their mind or heart, they have an unflinching bravery that allows them to have no limitations in physical ability during battle. They can jump hundreds of feet in the air, and they can scale a mountain with their hands and feet in minutes. They can swim underwater for long periods of time before they need to breathe. Basically, they can physically maneuver in any way you can think of that will allow them to defeat their opponent. The Clan That Knows No Fear are very formidable opponents and are led by Chief Bashwondo.

The Clan of Many Faces, as you may have guessed by their name, have the ability to shapeshift. To one untrained in battle this may seem like an unfitting gift during wartime. However, it is quite the opposite. When in battle, they can shapeshift into any form. They can become trees in the forest, or rocks on the side of the road. This gives the Clan of Many Faces an uncanny tactical advantage as they can catch their opponent off guard and give them the biggest surprise of their soon to be short-lived lives. In addition, they can shapeshift into their opponents during battle and only their other clansmen can see their true form. The Clan of Many Faces is a fierce opponent and is led by Chief Miyeen.

The Clan of Fluid Motion's gifts may not be as evident by their name but once you understand their special abilities, you will see just how much their name speaks to their gifts. This clan has the special gift to bend their bodies like water and move like the wind. Their motion is so fluid their opponents have a hard time physically striking them. Once they get moving the speed picks up like the wind. They can move faster than the eye can perceive and with enough momentum, their movement alone can knock their opponents off their feet. The Clan of Fluid Motion can take their opponents out before their opponents even realize they are there. The Clan of Fluid Motion is graceful in its approach and deadly in its execution. They are led by Chief Lashno.

The Clan That Sees Clear may be mistaken as seers. But on the contrary, they do not see possible future outcomes. Instead, they see their opponent clearer than their opponents can see themselves. The Clan That Sees Clear can scan your body in seconds and find every vulnerable spot on your body. This gives them the advantage to defeat you before you ever think about landing your first blow. In addition, they can also see every insecurity, vulnerable thought, and fear you may have and use this against you in battle. Due to the potential ability of being able to see into someone's mind being used for darkness, this part of their gift only activates during battle. If in the event of battle, the warrior attempted to use this against their own clan member, as soon as the thought comes to their mind, the Council of Sacred Magic will remove the gift instantaneously. Along with all of their other abilities, and erase all remembrance of any training they have. Leaving the warrior completely naked, unable to defend themselves in battle. In other words, the Clan That Sees Clear is not a foe you ever want to underestimate in battle. They are of the most skilled and deadliest clans on Eclanite. The Clan That Sees Clear is led by Chief Cashwahn.

Clan Strong Hold has the greatest physical strength out of all the clans. They can defeat any opponent with one blow. The strength they have also allows their skin to be like armor. It can be penetrated, but it is extremely difficult to do so. They are the clan assassins do not desire to take on alone. I do not know if assassins will be present during this battle, but if the assassins are present, I can guarantee it will not be Clan Strong Hold that they attack first. The assassins understand and know that Clan Strong Hold matches them in strength. The assassins are the one opponent I do not believe Clan Strong Hold can defeat with one blow. But, out of all the clans, I do believe they are the one clan that can defeat the assassins in hand-to-hand combat. However, if the assassins greatly outnumber Clan Strong Hold they would eventually ensure victory. Clan Strong Hold is the deadliest of them all and is led by Chief Sanyo.

—Thank you for the debriefing, Shemindsonlyone. This brief overview gives Kheira and I a better understanding of the potential danger we may be facing from within the Eclanite world. In addition to the imminent danger we are facing outside of the Eclanite world. Especially if the disloyalty has gotten into the warrior ranks. Depending on the strategy of the betrayers, this could trigger an internal battle which would leave the Eclanite people divided and reduce the number of those capable of battling the Kashnothians.

—Yes, Khogee, this is very true. I pray the disloyalty has not gotten that far, but we must be prepared for all potential outcomes. The disloyalty and betrayal are a blow to the trust I have in my Chief Warrior Council, but you know we have seen deceit before. This is not new to us and as a result of our past experience, we will be able to navigate this situation with grace.

Before we continue, are there any additional questions? I will take your external and internal silence as a no. Now that we are all on the same page let's begin preparing for our journey behind the veil to see the Eclanite Council of Sacred Magic. The first thing we need to do is sit in a circle with our knees touching. We will then all merge our energies together and place an invisible dome of protection around our bodies. Next, each one of us will breathe in deeply while repeating what I say. Remember to stay close to me and follow my lead once we enter the land of the Eclanite Council of Sacred Magic. And, no matter what you see please do not be alarmed or show fear. Let's begin.

Chapter 22:

Eclanite Council of Sacred Magic

— <Kheira, I can sense you, but I can't see you. Where are you, My Light?>

— <I am not sure.>

— <Do this for me, My Light. Breathe slowly and silence your mind. That is great, I can feel you. And in our sacred heart space, I can hear your heartbeat. Stay still, let me try something. Okay, if I walk east your heartbeat starts to get fainter. Let me walk west, ahh it is getting louder. It seems to beat louder to let me know I am going in the correct direction. Be patient, My Light, I will make my way to you momentarily.>

— <Khogee, you found your way to me.>

— <I'll forever find my way to you, My Light, even if you are in a different dimension. How did you see me approaching you from such a far distance when I couldn't quite see you just yet?>

— <I couldn't miss those broad shoulders if I tried.>

— <Seema, Dima, Kheira, and Khogee, can you all hear me speaking to you telepathically?>

— <Yes, Shemindsonlyone. Kheira and I can hear you loud and clear. Seema and Dima, can you all hear us? We have not heard from the two of you yet. Can you please report in and let us know the two of you are okay.>

— <Hi, everyone. We are sorry to cause concern. The portal we came through placed Seema and I deep underwater. We had to get ourselves to shore.>

— <I am not sure what happened on the entry, everyone. I have never had this experience visiting the Eclanite Council of Sacred Magic. This mist is so thick I've never encountered this before on any of my visits. Everyone, I am going to project a blue stream of light from my location to each of your locations, follow it to me please.>

—I am pleased to see all of your bright eyes again. I am truly not sure what caused all of us to separate and come through at different entry points. Kheira, did you all end up coming through an underwater portal as well?

—No, Shemindsonlyone. We were actually separated on entry. I came in through a portal in a huge tree. Khogee, where did you make entry?

—Well, I am not quite sure, to be honest. I was just in the middle of the mist and noticed neither Kheira nor anyone else was beside me.

—Shemindsonlyone, should we be alarmed by this unusual chain of events?

—You tell me. Remember your training, assess the situation, Dima. Let me know what you feel. Matter of fact, we will use this situation for further training. All four of you, take twenty seconds and assess this situation, and let me know if you all think we should move forward on our journey or return back to where we came and come up with a new plan?

—Kheira, did you decide not to participate in this exercise?

—No. Well, yes. I already completed my assessment upon entry. When I was separated from everyone, right before Khogee located me. To calm my mind, I became still and immersed myself in the present moment. As a result, I inadvertently tapped into the frequency of this planet and all I felt was a high frequency of love and peace. We are not in danger here. However, I feel we need to determine why the entry point is one you do not recognize, Shemindsonlyone. When entering the portal through the tree, whose name is Marigold, it felt as though we were entering one of the back doors to access this realm. I am assuming based on the latest development this means you normally access this realm through the front door.

—Your assessment is accurate, Kheira. We have brought all of you through the back door entrance versus the front door in case the Kashnoths' infiltration within the Eclanite world ran deeper than we realized. Please forgive me, I have not introduced myself as of yet. My name is Mosheenan, I serve the Council of Sacred Magic and was sent to escort the five of you before the elders. Before we proceed on this journey, I need each of you to step forward and allow me to completely illuminate your first eye. This will allow you all to see through the mist. Which is currently serving as a countermeasure in case anyone attempts to follow any of you through the energy stream you left behind while coming to visit us. As we are aware there are traitors amongst the Eclanite Chief Warrior Council, Shemindsonlyone, we took extra precautions to ensure safe entry for the five of you.

Now let us move forward with the process of amplifying your first eyes. As each of you steps forward, I will touch your first eye with the illuminated crystal at the end of my staff. Please do not be alarmed if you feel an electric current flow through your body. The magic and power flowing through this amethyst crystal will open your first eye up to its highest degree. When each of you has focused and tuned in, let me know. You will only be able to see as far as your perceived limitations allow you to see. This will be your first gift and will serve you well once you return to Eclanite and prepare for the war. Depending on your current bandwidth, this gift has the possibility to allow you to see beyond what you thought was possible—into galaxies beyond the reach of perceivable comprehension. With this gift and the others, you will be blessed to receive tonight, you will have enough power to defeat the Kashnoths planning to invade the Eclanite world. Now if you all are ready, please step before me one by one. Once I have finished amplifying the power of your first eye we will move forward on our journey.

Kheira, take three deep breaths and pull your energy back into yourself. I can see the energy you have taken in from my sacred staff's crystal is pushing your energy out, you can pull it back in. Wonderful! Quick learner you are, I see. Khogee, I can feel your energy and know that you are ready to move forward on our journey. Please continue to be patient with me. I have been listening to the rhythm of everyone's heartbeats in order to know when everyone has completely integrated the magical energy current into their first eye. From the current pattern and speed, we shall be ready to leave in roughly three minutes.

Before we continue on this path. Please know the council will only permit those who are pure of heart to come before them. Though I don't feel nor sense any duplicitous energy in your heart space, I still must warn you all. Once we begin to step through the veil that encircles the Council of Sacred Magic, if you are not pure of heart, you will be stuck within the walls of this veil, living out a time loop for what will feel like millions of years to you. You will only be released from this self-inflicted punishment when the Council of Sacred Magic says so. Let me search your internal thoughts to see if I hear any objections or sense fear from any of you. Seema, I see you have an internal pondering. I say the punishment would be self-inflicted because all members of any group that is escorted before the Eclanite Council of Sacred Magic receive this warning. If any member chooses to ignore this warning and continue on the intended course, they themselves are the only ones to blame for their fate. Ah, yes. I see everyone is at ease, with no more mental ponderings, and no fear. Proceed we may.

—Kheira, My Light, come closer to me I can tell you are cold. Come let me warm you as we walk.

—Thank You, My Light. Now tell me if your assessment differs from mine.

—Kheira, I feel we are safe and no harm will come to us here. You know if I felt otherwise, I would have objected as soon as you finished with your assessment.

—Yes, Khogee, I know.

—My Light, you have unlimited access to my heart space, you literally can tap into me whenever you please. My heart will always let you know what I feel and where my thoughts are.

—I know, as you also can tap into me. However, sometimes I just want to hear you speak. There is something about the tone and vibration of your voice that calms me, My Light. Can you feel the energy of this realm? I love how the energy feels. I can feel love and peace all around me like a warm blanket.

—Yeah, a warm blanket that isn't doing a good job of keeping you warm.

—Stop, I am serious. Look at these trees the way each tree is different shades of the same color fading in and out of each other from the top to bottom. I have never seen anything like it before. Look at that pink tree there and the different shades of pink that fade perfectly in and out of each other from the top to the bottom of the tree. I wonder if the colors signify anything. Look, even the animals adorn different colors. And, I can hear a slight rhythm in everything on this planet as it moves. Similar to how I can hear the sweet music in the ocean on Isonateon. Except I can hear it in everything here, it is all in perfect harmony.

—Yes, Kheira. I see you have been to the realms of the ancestors during your previous travels. Do you have any recollection of these travels?

—No, Mosheenan. I have no recollection of traveling to the realms of the ancestors before. How do you know this?

—Khogee, let me first apologize to you for interrupting you by speaking out of turn. Are you okay with me continuing?

—Yes, of course, Mosheenan, and thank you for the acknowledgement and respect.

—Kheira, I can tell by the rhythm of your and Khogee's hearts, that you are both in perfect harmony with the rhythm of this realm. Which lets me know you both have traversed amongst this realm before and have been endowed with a sacred gift. This is not the first time either of you has gone before the Council of Sacred Magic. Rather you consciously remember the encounter at this present moment or not. Once you come before them again, the previous encounter or encounters you have had with them should come back to you. All right everyone we have arrived at the entrance to the Council of Sacred Magic's abode. Once we pass through this door the only way we may move is forward. Does everyone understand, yes?

—Yes, we do.

—From what I gathered while reading all of your energy signatures, you all can breathe underwater. Once I open this door, you will see a tunnel appear, seemingly out of nowhere. This tunnel runs straight through the middle of the ocean. It looks like nothing is holding it together and that the water will crash down on you at any second. Know that it will not. However, as we move forward the water will close in behind us to ensure no one or nothing is following us. Once we get to the bottom of the tunnel, we will be submerged in water for thirty to forty-five seconds. During this time, our energy will be vetted by the creatures of the sea that guard the veil we must go through to meet with the Council of Sacred Magic. If you make it through the veil, you will instantly dry and find yourself again breathing via the air and surrounded by the lushest green foliage you have ever seen. Are there any questions? Yes, Seema?

—You say behind the door is a tunnel that is in the middle of the ocean, how can that be when we are standing in the middle of the forest?

—Come forward and let me show you. Push these two wooden doors open and let me know what you see.

—I see the forest and all its splendor.

—Exactly! Only I have the key that will allow this door to open right before the portal we need to travel through. Understand that any and all things are possible as long as you have the correct key to unlock that which you seek to manifest.

—Key? There is no keyhole on this door.

—Yes, Seema you are correct. Keys are not just tangible things you hold in your hand that unlock physical doors. With the correct keys, you can unlock the mysteries to the universe. Watch, as I demonstrate. In this case, my key is knowledge of sacred magic passed down to me from the Council of Sacred Magic. As I place my hands on certain key places on the door, at the exact right angle the door will open. Now Seema, tell me what you see.

—WOW, I see the ocean clear as day with a translucent tunnel glowing yellow and green, running down the middle. And as you said, the tunnel seems to be held up by nothing.

—Now everyone, before we step into the glowing tunnel, I have one last instruction for you. You must brace yourself while you step forward, as you will not step on solid ground. Under your feet will be a moving stream of water. This moving stream of water will serve the purpose of moving us along on our journey at a faster pace. We call this moving stream of water a kaklin. Once your feet are firmly secured upon the kaklin, the kaklin will carry you down the tunnel at a steady speed that will require no need for you to move your feet. The kaklin's are big enough to carry us in pairs. I will go first with Shemindsonlyone. It is best for Seema and Dima to follow behind us and for Kheira and Khogee to head up the rear. Though the two of you do not consciously remember traveling this path before, the memory of your journey is buried in your subconscious. If something were to go astray your instincts will quickly guide you into what steps to take to ensure all of our safety. As we all are gliding down the tunnel, the water will close in behind the two of you. Do not be alarmed. Excellent, everyone seems to be safe aboard their kaklin's and we are moving at a steady pace with no issues.

— <How are you feeling, Khogee?>

— <I feel wonderful. All of this feels oh so familiar. The gentle hum of the wind as we move forward is slowly pulling memories of me being here before, taking this exact same trip with you.>

— <Very interesting you say this, My Light. I feel the same way. My memory is being jarred by the colorful fish and aquatic life taming all around us as we move through this clear glass-like water tunnel. It is as if the creatures that inhabit this part of the water remember us. Do you see how they are all gathering close around us? Look back toward the end, they are all staring at us.>

— <Yes, My Light, I see them. But my thoughts were more along the lines of these particular inhabitants of this part of the water, as you so eloquently stated, are waiting to see if we make a misstep and fall into

their reach so they can have a meal. Well at their size it would probably be more like a snack.>

— <I can't believe you. The thoughts you put into my head. But now that you mention it, I do see larger and larger creatures starting to gather.>

— <Yeah, exactly. Look at this one over here. I've never seen anything like it. Seems to be as large as a whale, but somehow also has the head of an octopus and the tentacles to boot. This one is large enough to eat all six of us with one bite.>

— <Oh my, Khogee! Look there is another one swimming to my right and several smaller ones swimming behind us. Looks like there is an entire family eagerly waiting for their next meal.>

— <Oh Khogee and Kheira, please do not be alarmed by my size or my appearance. I am Cozthoe and to the other side of you, Kheira, is my wife, Kishmel. The four smaller ones behind you are our kids. We are here to do you all no harm. Quite the opposite, we are actually here as escorts. An extra layer of security as you all travel along the path that leads to the Eclanite Counsel of Sacred Magic.>

— <You are able to hear our thoughts as well as speak to us telepathically?>

— <Yes, Kheira, we are. Despite our appearance, we are one of the highest forms of intelligence you will find in this part of the water.>

— <How do you know our names?>

— <Well, Khogee, believe it or not, this is not our first time meeting you and Kheira. And, Kheira, I do hear your internal concern for the safety of our children.>

— <Yes, Kishmel. I meant no disrespect, I…>

— <Kheira, Kishmel and I hear no disrespect in your words at all. The concern you have is genuine and very pure. The type of security we provide is masking. You see, we admit a certain type of energy that masks your energy streams. A double protection to ensure no one is following

behind you all to attempt to enter where they should not. Our children are safe. No need to fear for them. Instead, you should fear for anyone who attempts to do them harm. I know Mosheenan has gifted you with a stronger first eye, to see beyond what you currently see with your physical eyes. If you take a moment to focus on your first eye, you will see purple dolphins swimming all around us. Just far enough out as to not be seen with the naked eye. These purple dolphins are sending a particular frequency to one another that provides a force field all around us and the water tunnel. If you look a little further out from them you will see orange shark-like eels swimming. These are the first line of defense. Usually, we do not need this type of security or protection for those traveling to see the Eclanite Council of Sacred Magic. However, this is a special circumstance. We must ensure the safety of you and Khogee at all costs, as your mission is of the utmost importance. For if you all fail to stop the Kashnoths from taking control of the Eclanite world, the galaxy you are currently taking residence in may be lost. And, in this conquering of theirs, we fear they will come to understand how to enter and conquer our realm as well. And for that cause, we are all willing to sacrifice whatever is required to prevent this potential end. Ah, and it looks like we have completed our journey successfully as you all have arrived safely.>

— <Thank you so much for escorting us safely to our destination.>

— <Khogee and Kheira, we are forever in your debt for the sacrifices you are making to ensure our galaxy is saved!>

— <Cozthoe, and we thank you and your family for ensuring our safe travel and arrival.>

Chapter 23:

Gifts

—I'm glad to see everyone made it through the fluid wall. I'm sure you all have realized by now I purposely gave you some misinformation. The kaklin brings you straight through the fluid wall and does not stop. This leaves the seeker no time to stop and think before entering. This is a safety measure against all who may not be entering for the right reasons. The fluid wall has a very high level of intelligence. It is able to read a certain energy signature within the hearts of all who enter to determine if the person is a threat, removing the factor of time completely out of the equation. From there, the wall will determine if one should be trapped within its confines, stuck in what seems like an infinite time loop, or if they will be allowed to proceed. Again, I am grateful that all of you made it through. Once we take our next step, we will immediately be in the presence of the Eclanite Council of Sacred Magic, please follow my lead and stay prostrated on the floor before their presence. You may only look at them and address them if they decide to address you directly. Know that they will not tell you their names, and when you hear them speak, you will hear them speak in unison. Is everyone ready to proceed?

—Yes. Yes, we are.

—Eclanite Counsel of Sacred Magic, we approach your presence with the highest honor and genuine pure intentions.

—Mosheenan, thank you for your continued service and leading our party safely to us. Shemindsonlyone, we are glad that you received our message, and took the necessary precautions to ensure a safe journey. Seema, Dima, Kheira, and Khogee, we appreciate you all for showing us honor and respect, by prostrating before us. Your effort is acknowledged, now please stand. We understand that you all need to return to your world quickly, as there are double dealings in the midst. To ensure your safety we will create a portal that will allow you to return exactly one millisecond before you initially arrived in our realm. This way if anyone is watching, to their eyes they will not see movement. It will be as if you never left. Each of you will walk through the portal as soon as we have completed our ritual. Though you will all leave this realm at different times you will arrive back on your world within a millisecond of the moment you left. Are there any questions? Great. Let's proceed. Seema and Dima, we will start with the two of you. We will make a circle of light around you. Close your eyes and relax. First, we will send gold light into your heart space. Then we will surround you with pink light. As I know, Shemindsonlyone has already advised you of the special purpose each of these gifts serve, are there any other questions you may have?

—No, we have none.

—Excellent, Dima. Now let us begin. I will talk to you both telepathically throughout the process. We will first connect to your heart spaces and will be able to hear your thoughts and tell exactly how much light you can handle as a pair without exploding. Once the limit has been reached, we will seal our gift with love. You will innately know once the ritual has completed, at this moment open your eyes. You will see a portal in front of you. Walk forward through the portal, and no matter how intense the urge within you, do not look back. Once you walk through the portal you will find yourself in the same seated positions you were in when you left, as if you never left.

—Kheira and Khogee it is now your turn. Your experience will be different from what you saw Seema and Dima experience. Do either of you have any idea as to why? Kheira, I can see vague cloudy memories swirling in your mind. Maybe you have an inkling as to why.

—Well, I know Mosheenan has advised that both Khogee and myself have previously been here before you, and just do not remember. Is it possible we have received these gifts from you all at a different point in time?

—Yes, Kheira, you have. Not only did you both previously receive these gifts, but you both were able to take in the highest amount we have bestowed in a very long time. We can tell that this light has served you both well and deepened the bond the pair of you share. We have watched you two for ages now, watching you develop and evolve. Observing the purity of your hearts and just how grand the love you have for one another is. We are highly impressed with your willingness to never give up on your goals, nor fall into the trappings of darkness all around you. You are staying true to your mission and will succeed as long as you continue to trust, love, and rely on each other. Allow nothing nor anyone to trick you into doubting one another.

Sama has seen your loyalty and the sacrifice you have made to get you to this point on your mission. He has approved for us to offer you a gift that will assist you in your mission as you move forward. This special gift will assist the two of you in safely catching up to the best part of who you are. He believes in you and knows that you are now ready to handle this gift. I see you have no questions or fear. As I feel and hear the peace within your shared heart space. Please kneel before us while we place a very unique energy package in you. Once we have completed placing this energy within you, you may feel a little unbalanced for a few moments. Please continue to kneel until you feel completely balanced. Once you are ready, please stand, and we will instruct you on the next phase of your journey.

I see you two are ready to move forward. You did a better job than I imagined while taking on the amount of energy we just endowed you with. Understand that the energy package placed within you will unfold over time. You needn't worry about the full unique nature of the energy package, just know it will assist you in connecting to and merging with the different aspects of who you are. As you move forward on your journey you will start to discover different talents and gifts you possess. Continue to maintain your humility along your journey, and know you must always have discretion and discernment. Once you start to merge and remember, there will be certain information regarding who you are, what you know and are able to do that shall not be shared with anyone other than each other. Everyone is not to be trusted and even those who come across as trustworthy may not have completely mastered the deficits of jealousy, envy, and covetousness. Do you understand the direction you are being given?

—Yes!

—Excellent. We wish you well on the next phases of your journey. Along your journey, if either of you start to grow weary or start to doubt your purpose, rely on the love you share and the strength each of you possesses. Know during every step of your mission you have the backing of the entire ancestral realm behind you! Now it is time for the three of you to return. Shemindsonlyone, thank you again for all of your sacrifice in ensuring this mission continues to move forward. Kheira and Khogee, remember we have our eyes on you.

Chapter 24:

The Tunnel

— <Seema, Dima, Kheira, and Khogee, can you all hear me speaking telepathically to you?>

— <Yes, we can.>

— <Excellent! I need you all to sit very still, do not make a move. Now that we are back on Eclanite, we need to continue to look as though we are all in a deep meditation for the time being. Now, I need you to focus on your surroundings and determine your assessment of our current situation. Kheira, tell me, what do you think?>

— <I can feel something is different. The energy of the environment has changed since before we left to visit the Eclanite Council of Sacred Magic. There is a presence here that was not here before. It seems as though the presence does not have the best intentions.>

— <Yes, I agree with your assessment. The presence that you feel, do you feel one or multiple?>

— <I feel multiple.>

— <Now remember Mosheenan enhanced your first eye. Use this gift and tell me what you see.>

— <I see that we are surrounded by a small stealth group of agents. The same agents the Kashnoths have sent after Khogee and me previously. They are hiding on the other side of the fence to my left.>

— <Do you have a plan to navigate this situation?>

— <I see that Seema and Dima have a tunnel in their basement that will lead us to safety. Once there we can regroup and move in position to

quietly get all warriors together and ready for battle. We just need to make our way inside their basement without causing suspicion. I say Seema and Dima should end our mediation since we are at their home. We should then talk for a minute or two about how calm and rejuvenated we feel after the mediation. From there Seema and Dima should invite us inside to make drinks and get blankets to enjoy the warm tones of the fire. Once we are inside, we can quickly make our way to the basement before they notice we have not come back outside.>

— <My Light, how do you know they will not move as soon as we get up or as soon as we finish our pretend mediation?>

— <From what I can see in the mind of their team leader, they do not want to cause a scene as all of their comrades are not yet here on Eclanite. After the exit we made from Kashnoths, they were very afraid of losing their lives to us. Instead, they would like to kill us quietly in our sleep. Without our presence, they feel the battle can be won swiftly, by the end of the day tomorrow. What I don't understand is how they knew we were here? How did the plans change so quickly from what Mohaneace originally showed you? Should we also question his loyalty, Shemindsonlyone?>

— <No, I do not think so. I do believe his intentions and motives are pure. I believe the Eclanite Council of Sacred Magic confirmed this by letting me know they were glad I got their message. I'm confident they would not have chosen Mohaneace to provide this message if they knew he had evil intent in his heart. It is possible since I changed my previously planned course of action, that it led to this present moment, as my goal was not to see you all until tomorrow. I believe whoever the disloyal is within the Eclanite War Council has better surveillance in place than expected. I know there was not a tale on me, and yet they are somehow aware. I'm sure they saw this as a prime opportunity to catch us off guard in our sleep. Hoping to take us out before the battle even begins.>

— <Hmm, they would be fools to believe they have any chance.>

— <Khogee, I agree wholeheartedly. Now Seema and Dima, if you have no objections to the plan Kheira has suggested, please, begin our charade so we can make a clean exit.>

—Shemindsonlyone, thank you for leading us in such a powerful mediation. I'm so glad you decided to surprise us with your presence this evening, it has been a true gift.

—Seema, thank you so much for the kind words. It's always a pleasure to spend time in the presence of my four-star pupils.

—Do we have your presence for a moment longer, Shemindsonlyone?

—Yes, I have nowhere else to be tonight, Dima.

—Wonderful! How about we all head inside, make some smoothies, put some snacks together, and grab some blankets? We can come back outside by the fireside and discuss our war strategy for the impending invasion.

—Oh, that sounds like a great idea. Do you have any strawberries, bananas, and a little honey?

—I believe so, Kheira. Come, let us go double check. I like where we are going with this, maybe the ladies can make the smoothies and we will make the snacks.

—Well, I'm not sure if I agree with that course of action. How about you and I get the snacks together and Seema and Khogee make the smoothies?

—Do you not trust us men to pick out the right snacks?

—Of course, I trust you all to pick out the right snacks, the right snacks for you. I'm coming along to ensure someone is considering what Seema and I enjoy.

—Wait, everyone, before we get started in the kitchen, let's go over to the linen closet so everyone can pick a blanket.

—Can you not just get them for us, Seema?

—I mean, I can but then I will be depriving you all of the opportunity to be impressed with my massive collection of unique artisan blankets, Kheira.

—Yes, please come see. Seema has an obsession with blankets. I had to build a completely separate linen closet just for her blankets. Which she makes me come in and view on a weekly basis. I'd love to share this thrilling excitement I feel when I view these blankets with someone else.

—Really, Dima? Just come on, let's go look.

—Seema and Dima you all executed our transition excellently! Now, let's hurry and move to the basement before they realize we are not coming back.

—Yes, of course. Follow us, the stairs are this way.

—Now that we are out of sight from our stalkers, there is a secret passageway they will never be able to find. Once we get into the tunnel there will be a room on our left that is camouflaged into the wall. I will show you all how to enter. There we can load up on any specialty items we may desire to take with us along our journey. I believe the uniforms you two left on your last visit should still fit the both of you as well, Khogee and Kheira.

—Let's make haste. I am sure they are already getting suspicious that there is more at play here. How do we access the tunnel?

—Yes, right this way it is over in our bedroom.

—First, Dima, please open the door to the linen closet in the hallway just a crack and cut the light on. This way they can think we escaped through the linen closet. Hopefully, this action will buy us more time.

—Great thinking, Seema. Now if you look right here behind our nightstands, either one will access the secret tunnel. There is an emblem embroidered on the back. Only Seema and I have the key to access this tunnel, the key is actually a sigil embedded in our hands. We have to place our hand over the embroidered symbol at the right angle and whisper the correct word to activate it. Then voila! Pay attention, everyone. I know it is very dark down the stairs so take caution as you step down. Once you put your foot on the first step the stair will light up, as will every subsequent step. This will allow you to see your way down through our path. If you are still unable to see, place your hands on either wall to your right or left, this will provide more illumination. As we continue through the tunnels, this will remain true. Any wall you touch will illuminate the way for you. Once we are all in the passageway the door above us will seal shut. The floor in the bedroom will again look seamlessly uniform, and they will never be the wiser as to how we disappeared out of this house.

—Excellent, I am very impressed with this secret escape tunnel the two of you have created. Most impressed indeed.

—Thank you, Kheira. Dima and I spent quite a bit of time drawing up the plans and even more time bringing our drawings to life. Your kind words are sincerely received. Here we are, this grand door before you made of pure marble is the entrance to our hidden war room. We will find all the talismans and artifacts we need to move forward on our journey. Similar to how we accessed the hidden door in the floor of our bedroom we will also access the door to our hidden war room.

—WOW, look at all these artifacts and talismans you have in here. And you weren't kidding, you do still have Khogee and my uniforms. WOW, how splendid and thoughtful of you all to keep these for us.

—Come on now, you two are our best comrades, there's nothing too small or big we wouldn't do for you two. Now please, let's all get changed. Shemindsonlyone, I'm sure we can find something to fit you in here.

—No need. I am always prepared for battle. I have my war attire under my clothes. I have my staff in my tote bag, and my protection talisman around my neck. I never leave home without it.

—Kheira and Khogee, before we leave, do either of you need any special talismans or artifacts?

—No, we are good, thank you so much for asking though.

—Are you sure? Dima and I have some pretty cool stuff in here. If you look, this bracelet here will build a force field around you in a matter of seconds. You just have to touch it in a special way for it to activate. This

ring will also provide an extra layer of protection for you. I can show you
how.

—Yeah, Seema is right. You may want to grab something. Don't worry,
Khogee, we have some manly-looking items over here that you can
choose from.

—Thank you all for the thoughtfulness. But like our training instructor,
we too have all of our items on us.

—It never hurts to have extra.

—I do agree with you, Dima, and we have lots of extra. However, before
we leave, I must add to Kheira's thoughts earlier. This is so impressive.
Did you all build all of this by yourself or did you have help?

—No, we built this all on our own with no help at all. And I sense your
concerns, Khogee. You may ease your mind. We have never brought
anyone this way. The only people who know this space exists are myself,
Seema, and now the three of you. So, there will be no concern of a sneak
attack or invasion as we make our way down the path. Well, if everyone
is ready, we can proceed on.

—Where exactly will this tunnel take us?

—This path will branch off into three different tunnels. Each tunnel will
lead us to a different place, the left tunnel leads to the War Council
Room. The middle tunnel leads to the Woods of Grace, or we can take
the right tunnel which leads to our old training facility. I suggest we go
to the War Council Room or our training facility. Where do you think
we should go next, Shemindsonlyone?

—Dima, I think it would be best if we go to the Woods of Grace.

—Are you sure? I'm sure if we go to the training facility or the War
Council Room, we will be able to link up with other comrades and safely
join forces with the other clans.

—I feel we should go to the Woods of Grace. If there are other agents
on Eclanite then the War Council room and training facility are more

known and likely to be invaded first. The Woods of Grace will be the safest place for us until we can decide what is all at play currently.

—As you wish, Shemindsonlyone.

Chapter 25:

Camp of Sacred Magic

—Mohaneace, what are you doing out here in the middle of the Woods of Grace, and in the middle of the night of all things!

—Shemindsonlyone, the Eclanite Council of Sacred Magic sent me a vision. I saw the five of you sitting in deep meditation with Kashnothian enemy combatants surrounding you, hiding on the other side of the backyard fence. I then saw you all in front of a path that had three branched-off tunnels. I saw each possibility and outcome of the potential choice. Both the right tunnel and left tunnel lead to an onslaught of Kashnothian agents. The middle tunnel, the one you chose, led to this moment where we are standing now. I was not sure which one you would choose, but felt your keen intuition would lead you toward the safest path, Shemindsonlyone! I am thankful you are still deeply tapped into your internal source.

—Mohaneace, do you have a plan as to where we can find shelter, and regroup?

—We can't go to the war room or the training grounds. They have both been compromised. This is where we would normally regroup. I sent out several messages on the wind's frequency to all the chiefs of our clans for everyone to meet in the Woods of Grace at our Camp of Sacred Magic. The message will disseminate itself in packages according to the energy signature of each chief. All of the elders who have been granted knowledge of the Camp of Sacred Magic's awareness and the key to access will receive a message of which chiefs and clans they are to bring with them. Just as those same chiefs who do not have access will receive a message as to which elder chief will grant them access to the Camp of Sacred Magic's secret location. As access can only be obtained via a sacred chant that will allow the chanter access to a portal for entrance. They should have all arrived by now and be waiting for us.

—There is another meeting site called the Camp of Sacred Magic here on Eclanite? How come Dima and I have never heard of this location, Mohaneace?

—Only myself and certain elder chiefs who have been in their role's time before times past were previously aware of its location and how to access it. The Camp of Sacred Magic is not accessible via a door like the ones we use to walk into establishments or places where we lay our heads. It cannot be located on any maps nor can it be seen by the naked eye. This location is heavily guarded by the Eclanite Council of Sacred Magic. They have protected the location by granting only the chief seer and certain elder chiefs knowledge of The Camp of Sacred Magic's location along with how to gain entry. In addition, only those with a pure heart and a triple-stacked first eye will ever be able to actually see the Camp of Sacred Magic's external location within the Woods of Grace.

—Why keep it a secret from the rest of the clan members? Especially the heads of war clans such as Seema and I? The heads of each clan, being the ones who actually lead the charge, should be privy to such information.

—This was a decision made by the Eclanite Council of Sacred Magic. A safety measure put in place in the event we were ever attacked off guard or there was betrayal amongst our ranks. The location to the Camp of Sacred Magic would provide a refuge for us while we regrouped. Each of the warrior clans' chiefs make up Shemindsonlyone's Chief Warrior Council, and we know for a fact there is deceit within the ranks.

—What is the measure to protect against the deceit amongst the warrior clan chiefs?

—Dima, I do believe this is why the Eclanite Council of Sacred Magic has chosen to only allow the elders of the warrior chiefs to have prior knowledge and access. They feel those who have shown loyalty over hundreds of years are less likely to betray. As another safety measure, once the dynamic message I sent to each chief is received the message itself will instantly teleport the chief and all of their clans' members to their designated secret meeting location near the Camp of Sacred Magic, but not actually by the Camp of Sacred Magic. From there, each group can link with the clan and the chief they were assigned to for access. This should prevent any betrays from having any time to warn the members of the Kashnoths army that are lying in wait.

—I understand, Mohaneace. Thank you for taking the time to explain this to Seema and I. Your words of reassurance really help ease my conscience, and understand the chance of this location being infiltrated is not likely.

—I am glad we reached an understanding. If you all would please come this way with me I will escort us to a safer location. At this location, I will access a portal that leads to the Camp of Sacred Magic.

— <Kheira and Khogee, can the two of you hear me?>

— <Yes, we can. Will Seema and Dima also be able to hear us?>

— <No, Kheira, they will not. I opened up a special channel on a frequency only the three of us can access. Something is not right, and in this moment, you are my two most trusted allies. Sama told me before you started training with me, that I can trust you two with my life. I too was able to see why he puts so much trust in the two of you after training you. The purity of your light shines through in the most beautifully humble way.>

— <Humble gratitude to you, Shemindsonlyone, for your kind words.>

— <Khogee, please tell me your assessment.>

— <I agree something is not right. Seema and Dima advised no one was aware of their secret tunnels. However, I find it odd that the only place Mohaneace sees agents at are the two places they were pushing you to choose for us to go.>

— <Right, Khogee. And the only place there are no agents is the one place they were not aware a secret location resides.>

— <Yes, I agree with the both of you. I have also registered these events in my mental rolodex as huge questionable events. However, I do not believe Seema and Dima are with the betrayers.>

— <Kheira, are you speaking from your emotions or from a true place of unbiased observation?>

— <I would say the latter, Khogee. Outside of them both being our dear friends, we know their hearts and intentions. They are loyal individuals who love their home. I do not see them being capable of this kind of betrayal. In addition to this fact, I feel they would have gotten stuck in the fluid wall surrounding the Eclanite Council of Sacred Magic if they were not true in their intentions. There has to be something much larger at play here we have not been able to see or figure out. It is possible since those are known locations of where the Eclanite War Council and warriors gather, they sent ambushes to both locations in the event the first team of agents they sent our way didn't succeed. If it hadn't been for your intuitiveness, Shemindsonlyone, we would have walked straight into an ambush. In addition, it is possible the actual betrayer themselves were not aware of this secret location and thus unable to send a team here to attempt to capture us. I think we should definitely take note of the inconsistencies of observations we have made and will make, keeping our intuition as our navigation system. However, I think it may be a little too hasty to assume Seema and Dima are with the disloyals. Keep in mind, Shemindsonlyone, they had no idea you were coming to their abode to meet us. How could they have agents at the ready to ambush us? From what you have said no one knew.>

— <Yes, which means there is a possibility I was under surveillance. However, this does not rule out the two of them being the ones who were doing the surveillance or possibly put the surveillance in motion. I do agree with your assessment, but I do not feel that Seema and Dima can be ruled out as possible disloyals. Let us keep our eyes open and pay attention at all times.>

— <We shall remain on high alert and guard, and keep this channel open and clear for ease of communication and strategic planning as needed. We now have possible suspects, whom I pray with the light of my heart are not the culprits. Based on everything we know up to this point I believe the disloyalty is deeper than we previously understood. There

may be a team of disloyal Eclanites at play here and not just one or two people.>

— <I agree, My Light.>

— <I know you trust Mohaneace, Shemindsonlyone, but what is the likelihood he is leading us into an ambush?>

— <As stated earlier the Council of Sacred Magic pretty much vouched for him. I don't believe the Council of Sacred Magic would have sent him the vision guiding him to our location in the Woods of Grace if he had ill intent. But with the current circumstances of the impending war and a clear mission to keep us from participating, we cannot be too careful. Now, Kheira, can you see ahead to determine if there is a problem?>

— <I don't know where to look as I am not sure where we are going.>

— <Remember your training, Kheira. You don't have to know where you are going to see possible outcomes of your future, warning signs to help you navigate your path. Breathe deeply into your heart three times. While breathing into your heart see pure white light radiating from your heart space up your energy path into your first eye. Once you have done this, set your intention on what you wish to see. When you have locked in, tell Khogee and I what your vision reveals to you.>

— <I see Mohaneace walking us to a clearing surrounded by all kinds of trees, foliage, and very large boulders. The foliage and boulders seem to be acting as additional camouflage and a possible deterrent to those who are adventurous and brave enough to venture beyond what they can see in front of them. Once we make it through to the clearing, I see Mohaneace opening a portal. Once we walk through this portal, we are in a huge room surrounded by the chief warriors, the head warrior of each clan, and all of the warriors who have come to defend and protect their world. Interesting, several hundreds of feet below this room I see a city. This city is currently being filled up by those of the different clans: the young children, young teens, the elderly, women carrying the next generation of Eclanites, along with those who are not trained for war. From what my vision is showing me, we are walking into a refuge. I also see a smaller room on the other side of the larger space that has access

restrictions on the door. I see that the room is empty and soundproof. This is where we need to gather with the chief of each clan as well as the heads of each clan to discuss the next phase of our mission. This way if there are other disloyals in the larger group they will not be involved in the planning. If there are disloyals amongst the chief clans' members we will have a smaller pool to investigate.>

— <I agree with you, Kheira. However, I do not think it is wise to have Seem and Dima in this room. As a result, I feel it would be best for you, Khogee, and the heads of all the other clans not to attend, this way there is no suspicion on Seema and Dima's part that we are onto them. This will also allow us to have a clearer line of sight to determine if there are disloyals in the higher-ranking clansmen.>

Chapter 26:

Battle Strategy

—Thank you all for gathering so quickly. Everyone, please take a moment to get comfortable. There are extra chairs alongside the walls if anyone is in need of one. Let us quiet down everyone, please, before Shemindsonlyone speaks and gives us direction, I would like to personally thank Shemindsonlyone, Kheira, and Khogee for their sacrifices. Their willingness to fight side by side with us to defend the Eclanite world, knowing that neither of them calls Eclanite home. Their actions speak leaps and bounds of their tremendous bravery and character.

—Thank you, Mohaneace. It is our honor to serve beside such noble people. I understand that an uncertain situation has very quickly turned into an inconceivable situation. I am in awe of the resolution and bravery the Eclanite people show us here this day. It takes courage in the face of uncertainty to stand and fight for what belongs to you, instead of running the other way. You all are a powerful ancient people full of magic and mystery. As we move forward on our quest to save what is rightfully yours, remember your ancestors! Remember the feats they have overcome, the strength they carry, and the fearlessness they have shown when stranded upon a newfound planet. All of who they are flows through the very essence of your beings. All of their magic, all of their bravery, all of their power. They will be your strength and courage as we move into the unknown. They will hold you up and fight side by side with you passing their special gifts and refined magic through you, demanding you push forward into victory. As we all know the Kashnoths have sent several small units of agents to assassinate the Chief Clan Members, myself, Kheira, and Khogee. Your ancestors on the Eclanite Council of Sacred Magic warned our chief seer of the impending danger, helping us all avoid an ambush. Further showing how much you are loved by those who previously walked the path you now trek. Hold fast, hold strong, and be at peace knowing we will not accept defeat. At this time, myself, Mohaneace, and only the Chief Clansmen will break away to determine a new course of action. The final decision will be communicated to all of you.

—Thank you to all the Chief Clansmen for being tuned in internally to the correct frequency in order to hear the message of imminent danger and taking the necessary measures to get your people quickly to safety. I know we are not sure how much time we have before we are overrun by the Kashnoths, agents, and potentially assassins. So, I would like for us to get straight to the point. Based on the recent events that have transpired I know there are disloyals amongst the Eclanite people. I am not sure how far up the ladder the deceit goes, and therefore I am very hesitant to let any of the Eclanite Warriors know our true battle plans. Do any of you have any objections to this strategy?

—Shemindsonlyone, I respect all of your training and knowledge as you have fought in more battles than all of us combined. I do understand you have an insight none of us may ever possess when it comes to the strategy of war. However, I do have concerns. If it is not known as of yet just how far up the ladder the rot of disloyalty has gone, are we sure we can trust everyone in this room?

—This is a great point, Chief Bashwondo. I do agree there is a huge risk with me discussing my proposed course of action with anyone at this current moment. I did keep this group small for a reason. There are only seven of us physically present in this room. Keeping the numbers small will make it easier to determine if there are disloyals amongst the Chief Clansmen or if the rot stopped before it got to the top of the tree. My plan to ensure we are not betrayed is to only provide the Chief Clansmen with certain details for our next steps. I know this is outside of my current style of leadership some of you have come to know, but the new waters we are treading cause for a different path to be chartered. However, I feel it is best to ensure the safety of the Eclanite people by keeping certain details from the members in this room until we know for sure if the rot has reached the top of the tree. Does the trust the Chief Warrior Council have in me run deep enough to allow me to keep certain details from you all? Wait, before everyone answers that question, I will step out of the room to allow the six of you to talk amongst yourselves, privately. When I return let me know what you have decided. Is everyone okay with this plan?

—I think it is a great idea but I don't think we really need to talk amongst ourselves. We trust your ability to see what we do not, and make decisions that are not rooted in selfish gain.

—Speak for yourself Chief Bashwondo.

—Chief Miyeen, do you have doubt in Shemindsonlyone?

—Chief Bashwondo, how do we know she is not the disloyal setting us all up for our slaughter?

—I agree with Chief Miyeen, that we should discuss being kept in the dark amongst ourselves to ensure we all agree first. However, I do not agree with Chief Miyeen on the idea that Shemindsonlyone would ever have the capacity to betray. I have fought with her before in battles and know she is completely loyal to the only one whom she minds. Sama would not have sent her here to assist us if the trust he has in her was not solidified and completely tried and true. If she is telling us to discuss our next move amongst ourselves before letting her know our decision. She is telling us this for a reason. I believe we should follow her direction.

—Thank you, Chief Cashwahn, for your wisdom. I will step out the back door and walk down the corridor to give you all privacy. Once the chiefs have made their decision and are ready for me to come back in, please come and let me know.

— <Kheira, Khogee, are you two there?>

— <Yes, Shemindsonlyone, we can hear you loud and clear.>

— <Is there anyone around you at the moment?>

— <No, there is not. While you all were deliberating, the ushers showed all of us our quarters, so we could meditate and rest until it was time for us to pull back together as a group. Since Kheira and I are leading a clan of warriors, we actually have our own room.>

— <How do you feel about the energy in the quarters you are now in?>

— <They are very comfortable. However, I am not sure… something feels off. I feel like we are being watched.>

— <Okay, Kheira, the three of us will continue this conversation in our heart spaces just as we are doing now. Are you all able to complete this task without it looking awkward or like you are doing something out of the ordinary in the event you are being watched.>

— <Yes, we are. Currently, we are lying down side by side with the lights off.>

— <Excellent! Were the two of you able to hear the conversation amongst the Chief Clansmen?>

— <Yes, Kheira and I heard the entire conversation, thank you for trusting us enough to allow us to listen in through the channel you have open for us in your heart space.>

— <Thank you both for being trustworthy, loyalty seems to be a rare character trait these days. Now I need the two of you to tell me your assessment?>

— <Chief Bashwondo, Chief Miyeen, and Chief Cashwahn were very forward with how they felt. I feel Chief Bashwondo is not a threat. His loyalty and trust in you were unwavering. Chief Miyeen and Chief Cashwahn, I question their trust in you, but I am not sure if they are the disloyals. I noticed Chief Cashwahn had very nice things to say about you, but in the end, her goal was the same as Chief Miyeen, to get you out of the room so they could discuss if they should trust you or not. She made sure to say how much Sama trusts you, and how loyal you are to Sama. One would naturally infer because of her trust in Sama that she trusts you, and is not disloyal. However, she never at any moment said she actually trusts you or Sama.>

— <Great observations, Kheira.>

— <Thank you, Shemindsonlyone. I will say for Chief Sanyo and Chief Lashno I am not sure. Neither one said anything, taking a neutral stance. This could be something or it could be nothing. However, their choosing not to say anything puts them on my watch list. I have learned one usually cannot put their full trust in those who ride the fence. Khogee, do you have any different thoughts?>

— <Shemindsonlyone, I agree with everything Kheira has stated. I feel her observations summed up well what I also surmised. However, we must not forget that Mohaneace was also present in the room. He also said nothing, neither publicly showing loyalty or disloyalty to you.>

— <Keen you are. Now tell me, Khogee, what do you make of his silence?>

— <I know previously he was sent a message from the Eclanite Council of Sacred Magic to warn us of impending danger and fulfilled his task. I do not see him being trusted with such life-altering information if he was not to be trusted. The only reason I could see him remaining silent is because he wants to make the potential disloyal think he is not truly with you. As Kheira put it, Mohaneace is outwardly displaying the act of riding the fence. Which could be a strategic move on his part to make the true disloyal or disloyals feel he can be swayed to their side.>

— <I could not have worded this observation any better, Khogee.>

— <I do have a question for you, Shemindsonlyone. What are your plans? How will you proceed if they demand complete disclosure?>

— <Regardless of the outcome of their conversation, the only two people on Eclanite who will ever truly know my full intent will be the two of you.>

— <How do you plan on fishing out the disloyals?>

— <In the vein of full transparency, this is all for show. I already know who the disloyals are, Khogee and Kheira. I too have been given sacred

gifts from the Eclanite Council of Sacred Magic. One of those gifts being the ability to read the hearts of those around me.>

— <Wait, so you have been testing Khogee and I this entire time?>

— <Kheira, come on. You should know by now that with me training never stops. I have an infinitude of wealth to share with the two of you, in the form of wisdom and knowledge. Therefore I will be training you until forever ceases to exist.>

— <Does this mean Seema and Dima have truly been compromised?>

— <I honestly do not know. Out of everyone around me, I cannot read their hearts. Which causes me great concern. The only person I have ever met whose heart signature I am unable to read is Sama, and I know the reason why I cannot read his. The frequency of his energy signature and the magic he wields is higher than any of the magic we know or have been gifted. The fact that I cannot read Seema and Dima's hearts puts them on my watch list, as you so eloquently put it earlier, Kheira. But what concerns me even more is the fact that, before we went to the Eclanite Council of Sacred Magic, I was able to read their hearts. I do not know if me now being unable to read their hearts is a gift given to them by the Council of Sacred Magic or if this is due to the works of the Kashnothians. And, I can't ask without raising suspicion that I am onto them. And, I can't ask the two of you to ask them. I feel if either of you do, the result will be the same as I previously stated. If they are not, this will put the two of you in a quandary to possibly disclose what gifts you received, which you both know you should never disclose. Those who can see, know. Those who cannot, do not need to know. But regardless the fact remains that something changed after we went to see the Council of Sacred Magic, and until I am sure if this change is because of the Council of Sacred Magic, Seema and Dima are not to be fully trusted. Before someone comes and gets me to hear the Chief Clansmen's decision, I would like to go over my plan so we can ensure we are all on point to cover one another as the time calls for it. Hold on. We will not be able to discuss this topic at the present moment, they are now ready to let me know their decision. I will send you all an energy download with my plans. If you have questions, we can discuss this in further detail later. I will keep this channel open so you can hear what choice the chiefs have decided. Remember to listen with a keen heart.>

Chapter 27:

Deliberations

—Your deliberations were swift. I assume you all must be very sure and firm about your decision with such a short conversation.

—Yes, we have decided that we are not in agreement with your decision to move forward without us knowing the details of your plans. With all of us being at the head of our clans, it is important to know the next steps. In addition, if something were to happen to you during battle we would be at a loss, and may not have the time needed to regroup.

—Thank you, Chief Cashwahn. Is this a unanimous decision?

—No, it is not. Myself and Chief Bashwondo do not agree with this course of action.

—Thank you, Chief Miyeen.

—I respect each of you for being honest and taking the time to put your home and its preservation before any personal goals. My plan to ensure victory in battle is to have each clan spread around Tafunut, the main power source at the center of this world. Tafunut increases the power of each clan as a unit by elevating the energy of the elements that heighten the magical abilities inherited from our ancestors that each clan member so gracefully wields. In addition, I know that Kheira and Khogee have been battle-trained in how to use all of the elements that strengthen each clan's magical ability. As a result, instead of having them lead a specific clan into battle as originally planned. I would like for them to act as floaters going where they are needed the most throughout the war. This will give us a tactical advantage.

—Who would then lead the clans they were going to lead?

—Great question, Chief Sanyo. I would ask that one of you volunteer to lead your clan into battle, or designate the next most qualified member of your clan to take their place.

—I would be glad to volunteer to lead my clan into battle.

—Thank you, Chief Bashwondo.

—Hold on before you volunteer, Chief Bashwondo. Shemindsonlyone, I do respect your leadership prowess and combat expertise. However, being that this is our home we are in danger of losing. I feel we should have more of a say in our battle strategy, as we have way more on the line than you.

—I totally understand, Chief Sanyo. What would you suggest we change?

—I suggest we change everything. Why would we gather around Tafunut? The Kashnoths could realize Tafunut's power is what feeds the elements that increase our magical abilities and destroy Tafunut. Which would destroy every Chief Clansmen along with the link each clan has to their ancestral magic. I say we spread out and allow each clan member to defend from different points of the island.

—Chief Sanyo, thank you for your willingness to speak up and let me know your unsureness with my battle plan. I have to disagree with your suggested course of action. To spread the clans out across the island would be spreading out our power, putting the clans at a disadvantage by removing them from the benefit of having their magical abilities amplified, thus setting each clan up for slaughter. If the Kashnoths realize the clans are spread out amongst the entire island and cannot quickly get to one another, Kashnoths could send their full force to attack each clan one by one, ending this battle before it even started. Regarding Tafunut, it is located below the earth's surface. Being that the only people on this world who know about Tafunut are in this room; the only way the Kashnoths can know or would know about Tafunut is if someone in this room told them. Chief Sanyo, is there something you would like to tell us?

—I would never be disloyal to the Eclanite people. I have no dealings with the Kashnoths people whatsoever, Shemindsonlyone. I am not saying they know about Tafunut. What I am saying is they could figure it out during battle and destroy it.

—Chief Sanyo, that is enough. Tafunut is a concentrated magical light source created by the Council of Sacred Magic. Tafunut lies underneath the surface of Eclanite and is protected by layers of magic, along with the power of every elemental that exists on this planet. Tafunut's energy signature can only be seen by the Eclanite Council of Sacred Magic and Sama; as well as the Eclanite Council of Sacred Magics Chief Seer, and the three whom Sama has granted the blessing and gift of being able to see Tafunut's energy signature. All those given the blessing to see Tafunut's energy have had their loyalty tried, tested, and proven true. However, in this moment your loyalty is very questionable. I would say you are having a momentary lapse of judgment due to fear, but your previously suggested battle strategy makes me question this theory. I know you are the youngest of the Chief Clansmen and have never seen war. Before you speak again, I need you to keep in mind that everyone in this room has seen war and been in battle, except you. Shemindsonlyone has been in more battles than anyone on the Eclanite World, including those who now reside on the Eclanite Council of Sacred Magic. She has never tasted defeat. Please show her the respect she deserves and heed her council and direction.

—Yes, Mohaneace, please forgive my anxiousness. I will follow the advice and direction of my fellow clansmen.

—Are there any other questions or concerns before you disseminate this information to the other clansmen? Is there anyone else who feels the battle strategy should be tweaked?

—No, Shemindsonlyone, I do not believe there are any further questions or concerns from any of the Chief Clansmen in this current moment.

—Thank you, Mohaneace. Before we wrap, we have two issues on the table that have not fully been decided. Who will now volunteer to lead their clans into battle, and will the full strategy for the impending battle be disseminated to the warriors? I know in this meeting we were going to decide which clans Khogee and Kheira would lead into battle. Since the direction has now changed, I ask for two volunteers. Chief Bashwondo, if you are still willing to volunteer, that will leave us in need of only one volunteer.

—Yes, Shemindsonlyone, I am still willing to lead my clan into battle.

—May I make a suggestion?

—Yes, Chief Sanyo, of course.

—With this being such a pivotal battle in the future of our world, would it not be best for each chief to lead their clans into battle?

—Chief Sanyo, this is not customary. If all the chiefs are lost, there will be no one to lead our clans.

—Chief Miyeen, I understand that in normal circumstances this is customary. However, what we face is not normal and requires us to take new measures. I know this is a risk, but if we lose our world to the Kashnoths, there will be no one for the remaining chiefs to lead anyway.

—Chief Sanyo, thank you for your suggestions. Since Chief Miyeen disagrees, let's put your suggestion to a vote. Who all would like to lead their clans into battle?

—I will.

—Yes, count me in. I am ready to defend our home to the last drop of blood falls.

—Thank you, Chief Lashno and Chief Cashwahn. Assuming your decisions have not changed, Chief Bashwondo and Chief Sanyo, that just leaves your decision, Chief Miyeen. Or do you still need more time?

—No, of course not. I will stand beside my fellow Chief Clansmen and will also volunteer to lead my clan into battle.

—Beautiful! There is much glory and honor displayed here today. We just have one remaining decision left on the table. What will be the course of action regarding revealing the full plan to the warriors?

—I feel that we should reveal everything to them except the fact that Khogee and Kheira will be used as floaters. We should present the change in plans as if it was the Chief Clansmen's decision to lead their warriors into battle due to the seriousness of what is at stake! This way we know if the strategy laid out for Khogee and Kheira is leaked to the Kashnoths it came from this room

—I do not disagree with this plan, Chief Bashwondo. I will leave the vote to the remaining chiefs. Are there any objections?

—No, we have no objections.

—Wonderful, it seems we have our strategy for this impending war. As the hours have gotten late, I believe it will be best if you all bring in each of your head clansmen who were designated to lead clans into battle. Take as long as you need to bring them up to speed. Once all details have been discussed, allow them time to relay the battle strategy to the rest of the clansmen in the early hours, instead of us waking everyone now. I will go locate Kheira and Khogee so they can be made aware of the strategy change. If I am needed for anything please come and let me know. Shemindsonlyone thank you again for your council.

—We are humbled in your presence and greatly appreciate all you have sacrificed to assist us in this battle that is not your own.

—Thank you for your words of kindness, Chief Bashwondo.

Chapter 28:

Disloyalty

—Seema, Dima, it is good to run into both of you. How are you feeling?

—Shemindsonlyone, Seema and I are both feeling a little anxious. We couldn't rest and decided to head this way to look for a snack, but we were just called to come review the plans for battle. I believe in the same room you just left, where you all developed the strategy we will use for the impending war. Are you not returning to join us?

—No, I am not. Before you go, do you mind telling me how to get to Kheira and Khogee's room?

—Oh yes, we are actually going to stop by there and pick them up on the way to the meeting.

—Wonderful, do you mind showing me to their room? I will brief them on their new roles as the battle strategy has changed due to the current circumstances.

—So, are they no longer helping us in battle?

—Yes, Seema they will help in battle, assuredly. Their roles have just changed.

—Oh, well, then it sounds as though we do not need to go visit the chiefs. You can brief us alongside Kheira and Khogee. I am sure if their roles have changed ours have as well, as we are equal in battle expertise.

—For now, Seema, only Kheira and Khogee's roles have changed.

—Really, Shemindsonlyone? I know Kheira and Khogee are sacrificing a lot, but they aren't from this planet, Seema and I can best them any day.

—I understand your eagerness to defend your home. Trust me when I say I understand how important it is for you both to ensure victory. Since Kheira and Khogee are not from this planet, the Kashnoths should not be expecting their presence for this battle. As a result, I would like to leave them as a wild card for the moment. You will be briefed on the strategy once you reach the chiefs.

—Understood! Let us take you right over and then we will head immediately to the strategy room.

—Thank you, Dima.

—Kheira, Khogee, I am about to enter, are you decent?

—Yes, please come in.

—I would like to brief you all on the changes for the impending battle. Once finished, I think it will be a great idea for us to meditate and ground. Now that I have briefed you both on the changes do you have any questions?

—To ensure a smooth and quick transition between battlegrounds, is the idea for Kheira and I to use portals to move?

—Yes, this is exactly the idea. Do you have any other concerns or questions? No, not at this time. Wonderful, before I leave let's have a silent meditation to ground ourselves for battle. When done I will leave the two of you to your rest, so you can continue to prepare your mind and soul for what I am sure will be the first of many battles.

— <Now that we are in our silent meditation, can you hear me here on our internal channel?>

— <Yes, we can.>

— <I know you all stated earlier you weren't one hundred percent sure if you were being watched or not, correct?>

— <Yes, that is correct.>

— <Has that uncertainty changed in either direction?>

— <No, it has not.>

— <Understood, we will continue to sit here in meditation and carry on our true conversation in secret. After listening in on the meeting, Kheira, do you now better understand where Chief Sanyo and Chief Lashno loyalties lie?>

— <I don't believe Chief Sanyo is a threat at all.>

— <What is your logic?>

— <A true disloyal who is working hand in hand with the Kashnoths would not be foolish enough to blow their cover, the way the true disloyal would like us to believe Chief Sanyo did. We believe Chief Sanyo is a decoy.>

— <By decoy, do you mean she is in cahoots with the true disloyal?>

— <No, I believe Chief Sanyo is an unknowing decoy. Being the youngest of the clansmen, I believe Chief Sanyo was unknowingly manipulated by the true disloyal to believe you were not capable of true leadership, and never realized it. We actually believe it is Lashno who is disloyal.>

— <Logic, Khogee?>

— <He stated nothing when you first proposed to keep the full strategy from the clansmen. He and Chief Cashwahn did not verbally disagree with your plan in your face. However, they did vote against your plan while you were out of the room. I believe none of the chiefs believed their voting decision would ever be told to you.>

— <However, Khogee and I think there is another disloyal in the mix— Chief Cashwahn.>

— <Please, do tell. How did the two of you come to this conclusion?>

— <We say this only because earlier, when we were in the common space, we picked up on a glance Chief Cashwahn and Chief Lashno made to one another across the room. It was something in the way they looked at each other that made us take note of what we saw. I also noticed when the seven of you headed into the strategy room, the two of their paths crossed and their hands brushed against one another. The brush could have been perceived by an onlooker as an innocent accident. However, it was the way they eagerly separated and moved in different directions that caused me to take note and raised my suspicion. After finding out the two of them voted against your plans, it solidified my suspicions.>

— <So, Khogee, you two think they are both disloyal.>

— <Yes, but we actually believe there is more to their disloyalty. They are lovers which makes them even more dangerous.>

— <Logic, Khogee? Why would them being lovers make them more dangerous?>

— <Kheira and I know all too well the depth a bond between two souls can reach. There is nothing in this universe that could ever make me betray Kheira, and no sacrifice too great to ensure her safety. When I observed their eagerness to separate before anyone noticed their hands brushed, I asked Kheira to focus on the two of them and open her vision and tell me what she could see.>

— <Yes, and what I saw is what Khogee suspected to be true. I also saw the energy surrounding both of them is not balanced in the light, which makes the match even more dangerous and volatile.>

— <Great observations, Khogee and Kheira. It is a true skill to move from seeing with your eyes to seeing with your heart and receiving confirmation for your intuition. I will confirm that you both are correct in your synopsis. They are indeed in cahoots. In addition, Seema and Dima are still a concern to me as well. Kheira, I understand you are loyal to them and completely trust in their loyalty to the Eclanite people, as well as you and Khogee. But something is indeed off. I set up a test for

them just now while they escorted me to your room, and they did not pass.>

— <What do you mean they didn't pass?>

— <They showed deficits I am not used to seeing in them, comparison and envy.>

— <I am sorry, Shemindsonlyone, I still do not understand.>

— <They know and understand that out of all the Eclanites who have trained with me, they are my best students. When I asked them to lead me to your room, I disclosed my intention was to update both of you on your role changes. They immediately started to compare their skills to yours and just knew their roles had also changed.>

— <You are correct, that is not like them at all.>

— <You understand now, Kheira.>

— <I do. For now, I will keep them on my watch list.>

— <Now that we have discussed this matter, onto the real reason why I have come to your room.>

— <Before we leave this subject, I have one more question for you, Shemindsonlyone.>

— <Yes, Khogee?>

— <What about Mohaneace? The other name Chief Bashwondo stated who agreed with him to keep your battle strategy to yourself was not Mohaneace. Is this not a matter of concern for you?>

— <Ahh, yes. Khogee. Now I know for sure you were paying attention. Mohaneace did not vote at all. He was there simply as an overseer. Since he did not have a stake in leading a clan into battle, he had no stake in the decision. This is an Eclanite custom. His role was simply to ensure everyone stayed on course and to take record of the meeting. Do you and Kheira have any more questions or concerns? If not, we can move

on to the true purpose as to why I am here. I need the two of you to deliver a message to Sama.>

— <Shemindsonlyone, I do not mean to show any disrespect to you in this moment by questioning you. However, I do not understand, the battle is on the verge of boiling over at any moment, why send us away when we can help tip the tides of this battle in favor of the Eclanite people?>

— <Kheira, the pureness of your desire to be of assistance in times of great peril could never be disrespectful. I do truly understand your heart and where you are coming from. At this time the greatest assistance you can provide for the Eclanite people is to deliver this message to Sama. Do you both understand?>

— <Yes, we do!>

— <Listen carefully to the following instructions. I need the two of you to wait until I leave the room. Once I am gone, create a portal with the intention of going into the middle of the Eclanite forest located on the far east side of the Tafunut energy center. When you arrive look for a robustly grown green tree standing alone as its own forest in a sea of green trees. As soon as your mission is complete return to the Eclanite world, contact me on our secret channel and I will let you know where you are most urgently needed. Khogee and Kheira, did you hear that noise? Kheira, I need you to look forward. What do you see?>

— <Kashnoths' entire fleet has landed. I see a red-light frequency connecting them to Chief Cashwahn and Chief Lashno. They do not know of this location just yet. However, if these two Chief Clansmen stay here much longer, they will. And everyone will be at great risk.>

— <Thank you. I will urgently move to the strategy room and have everyone move through portals to the West. I see now that Chief Cashwahn's subconscious is glitching. This is why she was so concerned about the Kashnoths learning of Tafunut.>

— <Yes, I can see it clearly, Shemindsonlyone. Lashno took advantage of her trust in him, he seduced her and subdued her ability to think or see clearly. While she was in a moment of orgasmic ecstasy, he allowed

the Kashnoths to attach a frequency to her and she has been battling internally ever since then.>

— <Khogee, now you and Kheira are truly aware and see clearly what is going on. Time is precious and running out quickly. We can discuss more on this matter at a later time. I now need you to wait fifteen minutes before you leave. Know we will be fully engaged in battle when you return back to the forest. I need you both to stay focused on your objective, move quickly to the safe zone, accomplish your objective, and hurry back to provide aid.>

Chapter 29:

The Message

—Kheira, My Light, I can feel you getting anxious! I promise we will proceed momentarily, together as a unit. Please be patient!

—I can hear the battle ramping up. The thunderous roar of warriors fighting with every ounce of strength they have until every last drop is squeezed out. Khogee, can't you hear their souls crying out, they need our help! We must go.

—My Light, we will move forward, I promise you. However, we must first get to the specified safe zone so we can ensure this message reaches Sama. If Shemindsonlyone has us leaving the war to deliver this message to Sama, it must be of the utmost importance. We will provide aid as soon as we return.

—I understand the importance of the message. But the battle is raging on around us, we must join!

—My Light, do you not understand that without this piece of info getting to Sama more than this battle could be lost, the entire war could be lost!

—I completely understand, and would never intend to jeopardize the mission in any way. Khogee, My Light, I cannot stand here and wait with you while those whom we know and have become dear to us are raging on in battle without us. I think it is best for me to go join those currently in battle. This way you can continue your forward movement to the safe zone in order to ensure private communication with Sama. When you are done contact me in our sacred heart space and I will guide you to me.

—Kheira, My Light, I forbid you from moving forward on your intended course of action without me by your side.

—You forbid me, Khogee? Who are you to forbid me from doing anything I see as just.

—Kheira, My Light, easy now. Remember who we are to each other. I understand everything you hear, see, and sense all around you in this very moment. Trust me, I understand the urgency as well as the pureness of your heart. My Light, right now I need you to balance the desire in your head with what you feel in your heart. Know in the depths of your soul that I would never purposely guide you wrong. At this critical moment, I feel very deeply within the core of my soul either of us moving forward without the other by their side would be to our detriment. I know that on your own, you are one of the mightiest warriors in the known worlds. Together though, My Light, we are the mightiest warriors in the known worlds. We are stronger together than we are apart, remember this.

My Light, I can feel in my heart space you are not receiving my words. I understand your desire to assist and I promise we will, but please understand everything must be done in divine order. My Light, come closer to me, look me in my eyes and place your hand on my heart. Feel my energy flowing from my heart through you, deep into your body. Feel the love I have for you in the depths of my soul and find peace. We have never had a struggle for power between the two of us. Please do not let this moment, when everything hangs on the balance of your next move, be the start! Trust in me, Kheira, the way you always have, and heed my warning, you must wait! For what we do from this point forward we must do as one!

— <My words will rise from the depths of your heart like a faint echo in the distance, and there will be no doubt or question in you, you must surrender!>

—Kheira, My Light, do you feel me!

—Yes, Khogee I do. And I apologize for making you feel that I no longer trust your intuition. I know you always have our best interests at heart. As always, My Light, I surrender to your guidance and leadership. Let's move forward with delivering the intended message to Sama. Once the message is delivered, we can do as you suggested, and move forward to battle as one.

—Thank you for always trusting me, My Light. I am not sure why, but I feel in my soul that your choice to wait for me has saved us both from great loss!

—Look, over there. Is this not the tree we are looking for? Didn't Shemindsonlyone say to look for a robustly grown green tree standing alone as its own forest in a sea of green trees?

—Yes, My Light, I do believe you are correct! This is the location. And I guess your temporary lapse of judgment was useful in some manner, as it helped us pass the time more quickly.

—Khogee, really? This isn't the time for jokes.

—Sorry, My Light, too soon, huh? Come here. Help me find the sigil that will open the secret door to the tree.

—Did Shemindsonlyone tell you there would be a sigil to open the door to the tree?

—No, she did not. I just assumed. How else will we get the tree to open?

—Per Asyihana, we simply must ask with pure intentions.

—Who is Asyihana, Kheira? And how do they know?

—The tree in which we wish to enter is communicating with me and letting me know the terms of engagement. Only those with pure hearts may enter.

—How are you seeing and hearing what I am not able to see and hear? I thought we were fully back in sync.

—My Light, we are. Come, take my hand, close your eyes, and breathe deeply. Connect to the energy flowing all around you and allow yourself to simply be one with all that lives and breathes. Now tell me, what do you see?

—I see the doorway for us to enter. Thank you, My Light, for helping me get centered. I always appreciate your guidance and leadership. And, thank you, Asyihana, for allowing us to enter your sacred home. After you, Kheira.

—Sama, is that you? How did we get here? We are back in the cottage in the middle of the ocean, how did this happen? When we stepped through the door Asyihana opened for us, we must have actually stepped through a portal. As she stated, only the pure of heart may enter.

—Yes, Khogee, you stepped through a hidden portal that accesses this location. Now that you are here, please hastily give me the message you were sent to deliver.

—Yes, of course. Shemindsonlyone advised us to ensure we delivered this message to you directly, 'By the time we planted our first seed, the one they'd previously planted had already begun to sprout roots.' Sama, I am not sure exactly what the riddle means but I was advised you'd know.

—Yes, Khogee, you and Kheira have done well. This message serves as confirmation. Thank you both again. I understand very well and know what steps to take next. The two of you please make haste and return to the battle, your efforts will be needed to bring this leg of the war to a swift close. Please step back through Asyihana's portal and she will ensure you exit in the exact location where you entered. Shemindsonlyone will be waiting to hear from you. She will advise where you are needed most in the battle.

Chapter 30:

The War

—Khogee, do you hear the screams in the distance?

—I believe we made it back just in time. Let's hurry and reach out to Shemindsonlyone via our secret channel in order to determine where we are needed at the current moment.

—Shemindsonlyone, we have returned after the successful completion of our mission.

—Excellent, Kheira. I am glad both of you have returned safely. Please make your way over to the Clan That Knows No Fear. Seema and Dima need your help. They are currently over in the grove of heavenly trees. They are facing heavy attack from a barrage of assassins.

—Assassins? They are here in this battle? They are usually only used for search and kill missions.

—Yes, Khogee, they are searching with the intent to kill. They are searching for you and Kheira. There are about twenty of them over there. So far, no others have been seen.

—Twenty assassins is equivalent to a thousand agents. This must be serious.

—Yes, Khogee. It is, you did kill one of the heads of the house of Khostempain, did you not?

—And I would do it again if it meant getting back to Kheira.

Thank you for the direction, Shemindsonlyone. Kheira and I will head to the grove of heavenly trees right away. Kheira, stand back a little, I will create a portal so we can get to the groove of heavenly trees quickly and expeditiously.

—Look, there is the Clan That Knows No Fear. Wow! Heavenly indeed. Everything is different shades of blue. All of these trees look like big fluffy balls of cotton, the energy coming from these trees feels purely divine and so relaxing. I'm amazed anyone is able to fight in such a calming place. Khogee, I am curious as to why we have never seen this part of Eclanite before.

—Kheira, My Light. Focus! Look, the assassins have Clan That Knows No Fear completely encircled.

—Yes, I see. Before we rush in, we need a plan.

—I agree. So tell me what is our plan of attack?

—I feel we need to attack from the air in order to have the element of surprise. We must make haste, as those assassins have Clan That Knows No Fear completely cornered.

—It looks like two assassins are about to put an end to Chief Bashwondo.

—Okay follow me, Khogee. I will swoop in from the left and you take the right. Once in position, I will stretch my staff over to you. When we descend upon the assassins, I will connect with my staff and turn it into a sharp blade. Let's decapitate those two attempting to slaughter Chief Bashwondo. Once we finish, let's create a small earthquake, isolated only to this area. I know Clan That Knows No Fear knows how to maneuver on top of shaky ground. However, I do not believe the other clans close to this area do. The Clan That Knows No Fear will all jump to the top of these oh so heavenly trees in one leap, and hold on without losing their balance. This will leave just the assassins on the ground. Once Clan That Knows No Fear is removed from the equation, I will create a controlled tornado isolated to this area. The tornado will suck up all the assassins, you can then open a portal to Kashnoths, Khogee. I will send them all back to their owners. This will remove the assassins from the battle, and make the rest of this battle a fair fight for the remaining clansmen.

—My Light, you are officially back. I think your plan is brilliant, but why not eliminate all the assassins now?

—Would the Kashnoths not just open a portal and send them back through to us?

—The Kashnoths have not yet mastered how to create portals on their own without the assistance of machinery, and we took the machinery our fake Kashnothian parents were using to create portals with us when we left. We could end their existence here and now. My concern is if we do end their existence right now, will our actions add to the anger and rage already being felt by the Kashnothians due to the actions we took in order to secure a safe exit from Kashnoths? Next thing we know a swarm of assassins show up in defense of their twenty fallen. I'm confident the assassins are still pissed as it is. We took out so many of them on Kaytoin, way more than twenty. However, we weren't worried about reinforcements showing up on Kaytoin as we were leaving right away. We don't know when we are leaving here.

—This is true. But the mere act of removing these assassins from Eclanite may still trigger an insurgence of assassins. Rather we annihilate these twenty assassins or let them live there is a possibility more will show up regardless. Either way, we are taking a risk.

—You are right, Khogee. Maybe if we spare most of the assassins' lives the survivors and their comrades may not get as enraged if we were to kill all twenty. Possibly slowing down the intensity of their desire to get instant revenge.

—Kheira, I agree. Let us move forward with your initial plan, My Light. Just make sure we are both thinking of another strategy to take out one hundred plus assassins in case there is a larger consequence to this action than we expect. On three we move. One… two… three, move!

—Shemindsonlyone, where did you come from?

—I was heading this way from Clan of Many Faces when I saw how quickly and swiftly you dealt with those assassins. Top strategists indeed.

—Khogee, you and Kheira showed up just in time. You should have let us in on your plan, we could have helped both of you with the execution. Maybe created a bigger portal to send the assassins back through.

—Dima, you know we would have included the both of you on our plan for their takedown if we had time. We spent so much time deliberating the strategy, we did not desire to waste any more time.

—Well, maybe we can execute this plan with the rest of the agents, and be done with all of this?

—I think that is a good plan, Dima. But the other clans do not know how to maneuver the way Clan That Knows No Fear does, in the face of an earthquake or tornado. In addition, I feel it would just delay this battle for another day. The agents would for sure return in full force with a better battle strategy, if we just send them through a portal.

—I agree with you, My Light. I feel it is best we fight the rest of this battle out and annihilate as many agents as we possibly can so the Kashnoths taste true defeat, and know the Eclanites are not to be touched going forward.

—If that is the case, what about the assassins, Shemindsonlyone? Will they not also come back?

—Seema, I feel if we can beat them here and now, the Kashnoths will not come back to this planet. I also believe if the assassins sole mission is to eliminate Kheira and Khogee the assassins should never return to Eclanite as long as Kheira and Khogee are not on Eclanite. But to ease your mind, after this battle is won, before I leave this planet, the Chief Clansmen and I will meet to ensure there is a strategy put in place to fight and defeat the assassins in the event the Kashnoths do return at a later date with them to battle again. As well as a way to contact myself,

Khogee, and Kheira within a second's notice of an invasion. How does that sound, Seema?

—I love this plan, Shemindsonlyone. Thank you. Now let us gather the rest of Clan That Knows No Fear and determine where we move next.

— <Khogee, My Light, can you hear me in your heart space? I still do not think they are with the betrayers. However, I do feel either we do not know them as well as we thought, or something is terribly wrong. I'm just not sure what.>

— <Yes, My light, my senses are heightened, I can sense you and feel you as deeply as I do myself.>

— <Did you notice how Seema and Dima came at us? Their actions are totally outside of the character they usually display.>

— <Kheira, be careful, as we both know all too well, that war can bring the best and ugliest out of people.>

— <Yes, I agree, and that is my concern.>

—Everyone, please listen up. This war is not over. The rest of our clansmen are engaged in heavy battle. As you know it was determined it would be best that all of the Chief Clansmen fight in battle to ensure our victory. We are all connected through earpieces, and it seems we need to return to aid the Clans of Many Faces. They need the most assistance at the moment. Seems the tides of their battle changed back in favor of the Kashnoths when more agents showed up to assist the ones being defeated. We will all merge with them and defeat the agents they are facing and then link up with the next clan. After each defeat, we will repeat this same battle strategy, linking up with the next clan most in need of assistance, until we have annihilated all the agents currently walking the Eclanite land. Are you all with me?

—YES!

—Excellent! Kheira and Khogee create portals that will place us right behind the Kashnothian agents facing the Clan of Many Faces. Once in place, everyone needs to close in on all sides so we have them encircled. They will never know what hit them!

Chapter 31:

The War Continued

—My Light, I know we are stronger together, but I must go over to the Clan of Fluid Motion fighting by the grove of purple trees. They are being overrun and need help.

—Yes, Kheira, I feel their dilemma. I really believe we should stay together throughout this entire battle. As you just stated, we are stronger together.

—Yes, My Light, but we are mighty on our own as well. Plus, we have removed the assassins from this battle. We make quick work of agents.

—Kheira, don't get cocky.

—You are right, My Light. I understand why you didn't want to separate earlier—you would have been in a different dimension while I would have been here. We would have been hard-pressed to get to one another in a quick manner if something happened. Here, we can quickly get to one another if the other is in need.

—Okay, Kheira, go. I'm sure we will be heading your way next. Call to me if you need me before we finish up here and make our way over to you.

—You know I will, My Light.

—Clan of Fluid Motion, I am here to provide assistance. You will soon be overrun and must work together to prevent this from happening. I need everyone to listen to my instructions carefully. To start I need you all to form a circle, starting from my right and left side until the last two members from the left and right side meet and take hands. We will fight outward never leaving more than four inches between yourself and the person on your right and left. I am not sure why your numbers are small, but know even though we are small we are mighty! Do not let the small numbers overwhelm you! Clan That Knows No Fear and Clan of Many Faces are headed this way as soon as they finish their battle. When I left, they were at the very end, more help will be here soon. Stay encouraged by the fact that you know you are not alone as your brothers and sisters will be here momentarily to aid you. In the meantime, stay strong and calm, wield your power from within, and show them what the sacred Eclanite magic is all about.

<Khogee, can you hear me? If you can, I need you! And I need you now! We are under heavy attack, and Chief Lashno is nowhere to be found. I am afraid the remaining clan members will not survive very much longer. I have placed a protective dome around those of us remaining so we can harm them but they cannot harm us. However, this army of agents has pulled out some kind of mechanism that is allowing them to break down the dome I have created. Khogee, I need you to watch my back while I take these agents out. Khogee, can you hear me? Please, come to me! I need your power!>

— <My Light, I am right above you. Look up. I'm coming down now.>

— <My Light, how'd you…>

— <I told you my senses are heightened, which deepens our connection as well. I felt you My Light, I knew you needed me. Why are the numbers of this clan so small? What happened to the other clansmen? I don't see bodies scattered.>

— <I'm not sure, My Light. We will get to the bottom of this after you help me finish the rest of these agents off. Come Khogee, place your forehead on mine. I need our combined power. Pull the energy from your heart into your first eye. Once it builds, send the energy into my first eye, I will then combine your energy with mine and make a power ball of light.>

—Wow, Kheira. I see the ball of light forming around our first eyes now. Now proceed forward with the plan, Kheira. Let our combined energy flow through you and continue to increase your power. Clan of Fluid Motion, please all take hands and stand in a line. We need everyone to grab the hand of the person closest to you. When the time is right, Kheira will open the top of the protection dome around us. I will send energy into each one of you so that when I fly up you will automatically fly along with me, be sure to follow my flight pattern. Once we are out of the protection dome, Kheira will close the protection dome around her. Do not worry, as soon as we are out of the protection dome around Kheira, I will create another protection dome around us to ensure everyone's safety. Kheira, My Light. We are ready whenever you are.

—Now, Khogee! Go!

— <You got this, Kheira. The dome is still holding, for now. All you need to do is split the ball of light between your two palms before these raging agents descend upon you. With one swift forceful move push the light into the earth and ask the surrounding trees to increase your power. There you go, Kheira, you are doing great!>

—Elemental Kingdom, I, Kheira, come before you with a pure heart full of admiration, love, honor, and respect asking you for assistance. Please come to our aid as we seek to defeat those who serve not the light but only the darkness within them.

— <Kheira, My Light, look deep within your heart and see you through my eyes. There is nothing but pure light surrounding you rushing through your hands into the ground. I see the light moving through the network of roots underground and rushing through all the trees. The Elemental Kingdom has granted your request and are drawing in more light! WOW! The light is so massive it is now exploding out of the trees and ground with such power that it has completely decimated the entire army without harming any of nature! The agents literally could not withstand the light.>

—Thank you, Elemental Kingdom, for assisting us!

—Shemindsonlyone, you all came quickly.

—Yes, we did. I received a call from Chief Lashno that you all needed urgent assistance. But I see you all did not need our assistance after all. Clan of Fluid Motion, where is your chief?

—After he made the call to you, he vanished. We have not seen him since.

—Chief Bashwondo, can you reach out to Chief Cashwahn and Chief Sanyo to determine if they are in need of assistance currently? Kheira and Khogee, while we are waiting to hear back, let's talk for a moment here in our heart space. While walking toward you all, I saw what you accomplished, no small feat at all. I see you both are truly in the fullness of who you are now. I just want you to know I was not the only one who saw. Be on guard against those who covet what the two of you have.

—Shemindsonlyone, I heard back from Chief Sanyo.

—Yes, Chief Bashwondo, what did she advise?

—She advised that the Clan That Sees Clear is with her now. They are fighting down by the silver water. Chief Sanyo said Chief Cashwahn reached out to her and Chief Cashwahn advised she had a small group of agents attack Clan That Sees Clear, and that they were able to take them down quickly. And would come to provide assistance to Chief Sanyo and Clan Strong Hold as Clan That Sees Clear were closest to Clan Strong Hold.

—Hmm, so most of the agents were focused on Clan That Knows No Fear and Clan of Many Faces. And I bet Clan Strong Hold is also being overrun.

—That is a great point you make, Kheira. Clan of Fluid Motion, what happened to your clan, as I do not see very many of them have fallen here?

—When Chief Lashno left, over half of our clansmen were frightened and also fled, Shemindsonlyone.

—Interesting! Thank you for your information. Please continue, Chief Bashwondo.

—Yes, Shemindsonlyone. Chief Sanyo went on to say that Clan That Sees Clear made it to Clan Strong Hold, along with Chief Cashwahn. However, at some point during the battle, Chief Sanyo noticed Chief Cashwahn was nowhere to be found. Chief Sanyo advised she has reached out to Chief Cashwahn several times on her comm device, but Chief Cashwahn is not responding.

—Hmmm, interesting. Did Chief Sanyo say if they were in distress?

—Chief Sanyo advised they are actually winning and do not think they will be fighting for much longer. Chief Sanyo advised us that she would let us know if the two combined clans need our help.

—Hmmm, even more interesting. Let's all take a short rest and then we will head their way to ensure the victory is quick. While everyone is resting, Khogee, Kheira, and I will walk ahead to the east to scope out our surroundings. Seema and Dima, can you do the same to the west? Walk no more than two miles and turn around and come back. If either party runs into a problem we will send our signal of distress, via a light sigil in the sky pinpointing our exact location. This particular light can only be seen by the Chief Clansmen, so please be diligent in your focus and awareness.

<Okay, by now I am sure the two of you know the drill. Internal conversation heart space only. Please tell me, what are your thoughts.>

— <Personally, I feel us heading to the Clan Strong Hold and the Clan That Sees Clear to provide aid is a trap. I believe when we get there we will be ambushed.>

— <I agree with Khogee. The fact that Chief Cashwahn delivered her clan to Chief Sanyo before she vanished says a lot. I doubt Chief Cashwahn merged the clans together so the Clan That Sees Clear could provide assistance to Clan Strong Hold. If that was the case, she would have not left. The fact her lover, Chief Lashno, has also vanished solidifies for me the knowingness that Clan That Sees Clear and Clan Stronghold are about to be overrun by agents. Chief Sanyo will end up calling for aid from the remaining clans, once the clans arrive and engage

in battle an onslaught of agents will appear out of nowhere. All of the clansmen knew the plan to continuously merge together until we defeated all agents. Knowing the plan for the clans to continuously merge was a prime opportunity for Chief Lashno and Chief Cashwahn to devise a plan to set up all the clansmen and annihilate the Eclanite warriors in one blow.>

— <Yes, I agree with you both. For this reason, we cannot merge with Clan Strong Hold and Clan that Sees Clear. However, we also can't leave them out there as sitting ducks. What are you thinking we should do, Shemindsonlyone?>

— <Actually, I was hoping the two of you could tell me your strategy. I saw the strategy the two of you put in place back there with Clan of Fluid Motion, I know you are ready for this.>

— <My idea is to send Kheira and I ahead. When you get back to the other clans' members, let them know we were anxious to finish this and decided to continue on ahead to assist in battle. Once whatever mole they left behind sees Kheira and I approaching Clan Strong Hold and Clan That Sees Clear, the mole can inform Chief Lashno and Chief Cashwahn. I am confident Chief Lashno and Chief Cashwahn will then inform the Kashnoths. Kashnoths can then start the execution of whatever plan they have in place. Once our intuition guides us at the right moment, we will cloak ourselves and search to find the agents the Kashnoths have hiding in the wings. Waiting for the right moment to overrun the Eclanites when the rest of the clansmen arrive to aid Clan Strong Hold and Clan That Sees Clear. We will contact you via our internal frequency to let you know where the agents are. I'm confident since the Clan That Sees Clear and the Clan Strong Hold are backed up against the silver water body, the Kashnoths are looking to attack them from the north. The agents will be hiding maybe half a mile away from the battle, waiting for us to walk in from the south. My thought to end this quickly is for you and the remaining chiefs to march the clansmen into battle. Once the battle is underway, we will create a portal for you to jump through and join us behind the agents. The three of us will work our way through the agents and thin out their numbers. They will never know what hit them.>

Chapter 32:

The Void

—Khogee, I can't believe we are here. Look at this. I've never seen a ship so massive, so wonderfully amazing. This room is so exquisitely exotic I could stay in here forever. We are surrounded by nature, under our bed is a running water canal that encircles our room. How beautiful, I can literally jump off our bed into living water, take a swim, and just relax. And we have to try out the shower later. Water is coming from every angle, all around you, even from the bottom of the shower. I was looking at the control panel on the shower, and did you know you can create different configurations of what you would like the shower to be and do? We can add seating on the wall if we require, I think a seat on the wall at right below your waist would be appropriate. We can even change the color of the water, add mood lighting, and change the mood lighting to whatever color we would like. We can add in a hologram screen behind the see-through wall to watch programming. We can also change the configuration of the shower itself to simulate us being in the middle of a waterfall or the middle of the forest taking a shower. We have been missing all of this while we have been on our mission. I am so thankful we were able to prevail and push through. We are on our way home.

—Kheira, My Light, I see you are beside yourself with excitement, and quite enthralled by this shower.

—I am, and Khogee, my mind has been visualizing just how many different places we can explore one another in this shower. But truly the most amazing part of all this is that I was able to take this journey with you. For us to successfully complete our mission and for me to finally have the time to lay here with you. Knowing that you are by my side experiencing the magnificence of this moment brings me joy. And, knowing you will be by my side for every mysterious wondrous moment that lies ahead brings me peace.

—I agree, My Light. There is no one else I would have rather completed this mission with than the best part of who I am. And, I am also glad we are finally alone. Now we can start where we left off on Kaytoin before we were rudely interrupted by those assassins. Do you remember where we left off, My Light?

—It's a little cloudy in my mind. Why don't you remind me?

—Come closer, put your heart against mine. Let your heart's rhythm sync with mine. Let's switch this conversation to our sacred heart space?

—Now that you are closer to me you don't have to tell me how the energy I'm sending you feels, because I can feel the pure pleasure and ecstasy running through every cell in your body. Now let's intensify this pleasure. Hold on to me tightly and don't let go. I put the soundproof setting on our room, so I don't want you to hold any expression of ecstasy back. Moan as loudly as you need. First, let me start by slowly licking…

— <Kheira, Khogee. Can you hear me?>

— <Yes, Sama, we can. Is everything okay?>

— <I need the two of you to get dressed immediately. Once you are clothed let me know, please make haste! We have a major impending problem!>

— <Yes, Sama! Khogee, I guess we will have to finish merging later, My Light.>

— <Don't worry. I don't care how long it takes, My Light. I'm going to feel your soul screaming my name while your body bends and jerks from the pure ecstasy of my touch!>

—Sama, we are here reporting for duty. What is the urgent matter?

—Shemindsonlyone and I have noticed something is amiss. Tell me what happened when we picked you, Kheira, and Shemindsonlyone up from the Eclanite planet.

—Yes, Sama. Once we successfully executed our plan and, the battle was won in favor of the Eclanite people, Shemindsonlyone had a quick meeting with the reaming chiefs on a potential strategy if the Kashnoths returned with assassins and how the three of us could be contacted for immediate assistance. Once finished, she advised us it was time to go home. Next, we saw a beam of light shoot down from the sky and Shemindsonlyone guided us over to the light stream. Our friends, Seema and Dima, rushed over to bid us farewell. We hugged them both and they thanked the three of us for the willingness to risk ourselves for the salvation of their world. Then we came over to the light stream and rode its frequency to the ship.

—Do you remember anything else being amiss or off once you got onboard the ship?

—Sama, I did notice the light stream stayed open until we boarded the ship. In my previous encounters with the light stream, I noticed that it starts to close in behind the traveler as you move up the light stream. I assumed this was a safety measure to prevent anyone from following behind onboard the ship.

—Yes, that is exactly right, Khogee. The concern I originally had was why the light stream stayed open and did someone end up riding its frequency onboard the ship. However, that question has been answered as I see Seema and Dima on this video in our hallways.

—Wait, what?

—Yes. Turn around and look for yourselves.

—Wow! Seema and Dima, why would they be aboard our ship?

—Do you remember the message you delivered me?

—Yes of course, 'By the time we planted our first seed, the one they'd previously planted had already begun to sprout roots.'

—Well, the frequency of the message you delivered was encoded with the true message. A safety precaution to ensure if you were compromised no one would ever hear the true message. When you stated your words my ears heard 'By the time we planted our first seed, the one they'd previously planted had already begun to sprout roots,' what I actually heard in my heart space was 'There is a chance Kheira and Khogee have been compromised, and I needed to ensure the safety of the Eclanite mission.' I knew something was amiss as you would not have been able to enter the cottage without being pure of heart. I then searched the energy signature of your souls and saw your loyalty was even deeper than before you started your mission. The message was sent to throw me off another's trail. What I couldn't figure out is who changed the frequency of the tone within the true message or how. Before you came before me through Asyihana's portal did you stop and talk to anyone?

—No, we didn't stop and talk to anyone.

—This is a mystery we will have to save for another day. For now, we need to address the issue before us.

—Sama, it is hard to grasp that Seema and Dima would betray their own people. They love them dearly.

—I agree, Kheira, so tell me what do you think is really going on? Because the Seema and Dima I know would not do this either. It is not in their soul signature to complete this type of betrayal. Was there ever a time when the two of you were not around Seema and Dima?

—Yes, there were several times we were not in their presence. The first time was when we left the realm the Eclanite Council of Sacred Magic resides in. They went through a portal to return to Eclanite and we left the Eclanite Council of Sacred Mage fifteen minutes after them, but returned to Eclanite within a millisecond of the time they arrived on Eclanite.

—Are you sure there were no other unaccounted moments that stand out, Khogee?

—I am not sure, Sama. I cannot say for sure. What I can say is that they were acting very differently when we returned. I noticed the change in their personality when they attempted to persuade us to take one of their artifacts. However much Kheira and I love and trust Seema and Dima, we remember our training and know while on this mission not to take anything of the such from anyone but you or Shemindsonlyone, Sama. The next strange thing was the way it seemed they were attempting to manipulate the choice Shemindsonlyone would make as to where we would go for sanctuary until we determined our next move. To the point you were making, Sama, it is very possible there were moments unaccounted for once we left the Eclanite Council of Sacred Magic?

—If this theory holds weight, then it is possible those are not our Seema and Dima roaming these hallways. Similar to how the Kashnoths implanted a fake you in the restaurant on Saynohs to take me out.

—Yes, Kheira, My Light, I agree. And if this is the case, where is the real Seema and Dima?

—Now we must hunt them down and get them off this ship. Kheira and I will move about the ship to locate and bring in the threat for questioning.

—I will also have small groups of warriors move through the ship to locate the threat. If any group of warriors locate the threat before you and Kheira do, they will radio to you and Kheira to meet them at their location so you can bring them in.

—This is an excellent plan, Shemindsonlyone. Let us move.

—Ahh, Kheira and Khogee. I see the two of you are in your war attire. How fitting. I assume you were coming to look for us. No, need as we have been looking for you. Now we will finish what started on Kashnoths.

—What do you mean finish what started on Kashnoths? You were not there?

—Kheira, watch out.

—Khogee, wait. Where did you go? What is this, imposters? Why is there nothing but a dark hole where Khogee once stood.

—Well, we were attempting to put you there, but Khogee jumped in the way. Oh well, as long as the two of you are separated, we have attenuated your power.

—Answer me now, where is Khogee!

—He is in a void where he will stay beyond the point where time ends.

— <Kheira, My Light, can you hear me here in your heart space?>

— <Yes, Khogee, I can.>

— <I feel this connection will die soon. Know that nothing will ever keep me from you. I will come to you, My Light. I love you with all that I am.>

— <Khogee, I can't let you go like this. I refuse to lose you again not knowing when our paths will cross.>

— <You will never lose me, My Light! We are bound to one another beyond infinity. I will always find you, My Light. This will just be another short separation.>

—Kheira, what is going on? Where is Khogee?

—They threw him in this void. And as most do when in a moment of arrogance, they said too much and underestimated the bond Khogee and I share. Shemindsonlyone, I will see you on the other side.

—Kheira, wait. No, don't go in there!

—Wow, I didn't expect her to jump in the void as well. It doesn't matter at this point. We have fulfilled our mission.

—Yes, we have, Dima. However, I do wonder what she meant by we said too much.

—Does it matter? We will never see them again. There is no way for them to get out of where they are.

—Take them into custody immediately!

—Do as you will. We have fulfilled our purpose and are completely at peace with being taken all the way offline.

—Kheira, what have you done! Why did you jump in here!

—My Light, I can't bear losing you again. And as you have said before, 'what we do from this point forward we must do as one!' Plus, that fake pair of Dima and Seema showed their hands. They said they needed to separate us in order to attenuate our power. So, if their goal was to separate us, my goal was to keep us together. This was also the same plan as the royals on Kashnoths, Khogee. I know you didn't want me to follow you, My Light. But there is a reason our enemies want to keep us separated. For this reason, we must do all we can to ensure they never succeed. Now let's figure a way out of this void, so we can end this war once and for all. The Kashnoths planet has no idea what they have done or what they are in store for. We will wipe their existence out of the galaxies.

Pronunciation Guide

People

Khogee — Kho-g

Kheira — Khe-ruh

Yemeya — Yeh-me-ya

Mishona — Me-sho-na

Shinaya — Shu-ni-ya

Alcarekh — Al-cuh-rek

Aynobe — A-no-bee

Lanrete Retsam — Lan-ret / Ret-sum

Ashbanke — Ash-bank

Khanestine — Can-eh-stine

Kheynoos — Key-nose

Khostempain — Co-stem-pain

Khininten — Kin-in-ten

General Tathanboth — Ta-than-bahth

Shemindsonlyone — She-minds-only-one

Sama — Sah-muh

Seema — See-ma

Dima — Deh-ma

Theonewhoquestions — The-one-who-questions

Mohaneace — Mow-ah-niece

Chief Bashwondo — Bash-wand-o

Chief Miyeen — My-een

Chief Lashno — Lash-no

Chief Cashwahn — Cash-waan

Chief Sanyo — San-yo

Mosheenan — Mo-sheen-an

Cozthoe — Coze-toe

Kishmel — Kish-mel

Asyihana — As-uh-niya

Planets/Worlds/Places

Planet Kaytoin — K-toyn

Planet Moriahn — Mo-rye-an

Planet Saynohs — Say-nose

Planet Ninotah — Ninah-taw

Planet Kashnoths — Cash-noths

Planet Isonateon — Iso-nate-un

Eclanite — Ek-la-nite

Trivarious Mountains —Try-various

Tafunut — Taf-uh-nut

Groups of People

Kashnothians — Cash-no-the-uns

Isonateon — Iso-nate-un

Eclanites — Ek-la-nites

Saynohtians —Say-no-te-un

Houses

House of Sekhmet — Sek-met

House of Anpu — Ahn-pooh

House of Khininten — Ken-in-ten

House of Khostempain — Co-stem-pain

Other Terms

Kaklin — Kak-lynn

Thank You For Reading My Book!

I really appreciate all of your feedback and I love hearing what you have to say. Please take a moment to leave a helpful review on your favorite book platform letting me know what you thought of the book.

www.amandaevansauthor.com/reviews

Thanks so much!

-Amanda Evans

About the Author

Amanda Evans is an award-winning author. Her literary journey started with poetry, culminating in the publication of her poetry book, Thoughts in the Meantime. Since then, she has transitioned into exploring deeper connections and mysteries of our universe, leading her to write *Kheira & Khogee: The Legend Begins*. When she steps away from writing, Amanda cherishes every opportunity to connect with family and friends on a deeper level, all while fostering a greater sense of self.

Stay updated on Amanda's next book release by joining her mailing list for news, fun giveaways, insider scoops, and more!

Sign up and contact her at **www.amandaevansauthor.com.**